They'd been friends, then lovers. But never again...

"What are you so afraid of?"

"Don't, Jon. You know what happened to our friendship the last time we... The last time."

Jon's eyebrows lifted ironically. "Sorry it was such an unpleasant experience for you."

Angela's face reddened.

Jon studied her thoughtfully. "Aren't you at all curious about this attraction between us? Where it's coming from? Where it's going?"

"I know where it's going! That's what I'm trying to head off. We're friends again—finally. But it took nine years. Next time, I'm afraid forever won't be long enough to heal the breach."

Shannon Waverly lives in Massachusetts with her husband, a high school English teacher. She wrote her first romance at the age of twelve, and Shannon's been writing ever since. She says that in her first year of college, she joined the literary magazine and "promptly submitted the most pompous allegory imaginable. The editor at the time just as promptly rejected it. But he also asked me out. He and I have now been married for over twenty-one years."

Books by Shannon Waverly

HARLEQUIN ROMANCE
3072–A SUMMER KIND OF LOVE
3150–NO TRESPASSING
3204–NEW LEASE ON LOVE
3259–TEMPORARY ARRANGEMENT

Don't miss any of our special offers. Write to us at the following address for information on our newest releases.

Harlequin Reader Service
P.O. Box 1397, Buffalo, NY 14240
Canadian address: P.O. Box 603,
Fort Erie, Ont. L2A 5X3

CHRISTMAS ANGEL
Shannon Waverly

Harlequin Books

TORONTO • NEW YORK • LONDON
AMSTERDAM • PARIS • SYDNEY • HAMBURG
STOCKHOLM • ATHENS • TOKYO • MILAN
MADRID • WARSAW • BUDAPEST • AUCKLAND

If you purchased this book without a cover you should be aware that this book is stolen property. It was reported as "unsold and destroyed" to the publisher, and neither the author nor the publisher has received any payment for this "stripped book."

This book is dedicated to my father, who passed away during its writing

Miss you, Dad

ISBN 0-373-03292-7

CHRISTMAS ANGEL

Copyright © 1993 by Kathleen Shannon.

All rights reserved. Except for use in any review, the reproduction or utilization of this work in whole or in part in any form by any electronic, mechanical or other means, now known or hereafter invented, including xerography, photocopying and recording, or in any information storage or retrieval system, is forbidden without the written permission of the publisher, Harlequin Enterprises Limited, 225 Duncan Mill Road, Don Mills, Ontario, Canada M3B 3K9.

All characters in this book have no existence outside the imagination of the author and have no relation whatsoever to anyone bearing the same name or names. They are not even distantly inspired by any individual known or unknown to the author, and all incidents are pure invention.

This edition published by arrangement with Harlequin Enterprises B. V.

® and TM are trademarks of the publisher. Trademarks indicated with ® are registered in the United States Patent and Trademark Office, the Canadian Trade Marks Office and in other countries.

Printed in U.S.A.

CHAPTER ONE

ANGELA CAME TO with a start, realizing the music around her had subsided.

"Where were you, Miss Westgate?" Mr. Beech inquired.

Embarrassment climbed up her cheeks like mercury in a thermometer. Usually she didn't make mistakes, and *never* two weeks before a concert.

"All right, let's pick it up at the top of page seven, third bar." The white-maned conductor tapped his baton, and Angela raised her flute, determined to concentrate extra hard on her playing—which was what she should have been doing, not thinking about her argument with Ivan.

It was unlike her to let personal problems interfere with rehearsal. Just the opposite, rehearsal usually calmed whatever ailed her. But apparently today's argument had dug in deeper than she'd realized. It was the same one they'd been having on and off for a couple of weeks now. Why couldn't their relationship take a step forward? he wanted to know. Why couldn't he move into her place?

She'd repeated the answer she'd given him on the other occasions when the issue had arisen: she wasn't capable of making a decision of that magnitude at this particular juncture of her life. She couldn't think straight. She was too keyed up waiting to hear if she'd be named Mr. Beech's successor. Maybe in a month, after the appointment was made...

But Ivan had kept pressing until finally she'd agreed to give the matter serious thought and get back to him with a definite decision by the weekend.

She'd eventually got him out the door, but hadn't been able to return to the Christmas cards she'd been writing before his arrival. Instead, she'd curled up in a wing chair by her empty fireplace, wrapped in an afghan her mother had finished crocheting just a month before she'd died, and for the rest of the afternoon wondered why she couldn't give the man she supposedly loved a simple affirmative answer.

Angela tensed as the orchestra approached the passage she'd missed a few minutes earlier. This time her playing was flawless.

On an objective level, she had no trouble understanding Ivan's impatience to move in. They *had* been seeing each other exclusively for nearly half a year. Sharing expenses *would* save them money. And it *would* be nice to spend the holiday season together.

Still, Angela couldn't help feeling rushed—and resentful—which only added to her sense of guilt. But, damn it all, it didn't seem fair, Ivan's putting such pressure on her right now. Directorship of the Winston Symphony Orchestra meant everything to her.

She fully realized that to an outsider the WSO was probably just one more unremarkable community orchestra, but to her it was home. Her center. Her source of energy and emotional healing. She didn't know why this was so. She had other jobs to satisfy her love of music, jobs, unlike this one, that paid more than a token salary. But she was never quite as happy at her other pursuits as she was here.

And Ivan knew it, too. He also knew how frightened she was that she wouldn't get the position. And who knew when it would open up again? Mr. Beech had been at the helm for thirty-five years. The new conductor might very well do the same.

Angela's résumé was good. She had the right training, a broad range of experience—including being Mr. Beech's assistant for the past three years—and she'd certainly paid her dues. She'd been with the orchestra for seven years, having joined while still in college, had never missed a rehearsal and served on more committees than she cared to remember. She wasn't just qualified; she *deserved* the position, yet she knew the board of directors might easily arrive at a different conclusion.

For one thing, she was a woman, and the idea of a female conductor was probably as foreign to the small town of Winston, New Hampshire, as a Martian running for tax assessor. The board might also dismiss her application simply because she was a local, perversely reasoning that no one from the area could possibly be good.

Angela's deepest fear, however, was that someone better qualified had also applied for the job. It was precisely this uncertainty, this not knowing who her competition was, that was turning her into a certifiable tangle of nerves, and Ivan had no right throwing yet another worry onto the heap!

The last triumphant notes of the Jupiter Symphony reverberated around the red velvet curtains and gilded cornices of the theater, then faded in a series of diminishing after-echoes. Angela smiled, ripples of pleasure running along her arms.

With long knob-knuckled hands, Mr. Beech smoothed back his thick hair. "That was good. Very nice," he said, which was as profuse as he got with his compliments. "Let's proceed, then, to the sing-along carol medley."

Angela bent forward, searching for the folder of sheet music under her chair. While she was down there, a shiver raced down her back, causing her to wonder if someone had opened a door offstage, letting in a draft. But then the shiver changed, deepened, and Angela went very still. She swallowed, hardly breathing, as the sensation became a visceral awareness—of something. Something out in the dark center aisle. Without straightening, she lifted her gaze just as that something moved into the arc of light cast from the stage. First, she noticed brown leather boots, broken in and mellow, then long lean legs molded by faded denim jeans and, as her eyes continued to lift, a black French-horn case gripped in a leather-gloved hand. Her heart pounded, and her impatient gaze flew to the newcomer's face.

"Merciful Mozart!" Angela breathed. She sat up, moving as if the stage lights were suddenly pouring down thick warm molasses. Everything around her faded to nothing, leaving her with only one all-consuming awareness. Jon!

He paused at the first row of seats, carefully set his instrument case on the floor, unzipped his brown leather jacket and took the aisle seat.

"Oh, my!" the girl beside Angela sighed. She'd apparently been watching his entrance, too. "What do we have here?"

What indeed? Angela thought, gripping her arms tight in an attempt to control their trembling. Jonathan Stoddard couldn't be explained in a minute, nor in an hour. Maybe not at all. Jon was one of those rare individuals better defined as a force of nature, like spontaneous combustion or winter lightning.

For years, he'd also been her very best friend.

But that was all so long ago, before college separated them, before his family moved away. So many years had passed since they'd even seen each other that Angela had begun to believe they'd never meet again.

But there he was. And though she was absolutely overwhelmed and had no idea what a world-class performer was doing at a small-town orchestra rehearsal in southern New Hampshire on a cold December Wednesday, she also felt the oddest sensation of a thread unbroken. His appearance was both the most startling occurrence in her life and yet the most natural.

Someone in the cello section caught the elderly conductor's attention and pointed. He turned from his podium.

"Ah, Jonathan!" Mr. Beech hobbled across the stage and down the side steps, a smile crinkling unfamiliar lines into his face. They shook hands and spoke quietly while a hush of curiosity fell over the musicians on stage.

The girl beside Angela sighed again. "I think I'm in love."

Angela chuckled because that was the expected response, but the reality of the situation was just sinking home. Oh, Lord, oh, Lord! This couldn't be happening! Jon wasn't really here, was he? She closed her eyes and with all her might willed him to disappear. But when she peeked through her lashes a few seconds later he was still there, looking more forceful and vibrant than ever.

Growing up, Angela hadn't paid much attention to Jon's looks. He'd always been just Jon to her, the boy she'd known since before she could cross the street on her own. Just Jon, who'd played space cadets with her and grumbled over starched recital clothes and shared her case of chicken pox. But somewhere around the age of fifteen, she'd become aware of his entourage, those flocks of pea-brained girls panting after him down the corridors of Winston High or parading their wares in front of the stage whenever the band played an engagement. It was then that she'd taken an objective look and grudgingly admitted that, yes, her best friend was indeed a heartbreaker.

Now, unable to bridle her curiosity, Angela peered around the musician in front of her to get a better look. As usual, Jon needed a haircut, his coarse, nearly black curls springing about his handsome face with rakish abandon. And he still refused to dress professionally.

But time had changed him, too, she noticed. He was broader in the shoulders, thicker in the thighs, the coltish beauty of his youth transformed into something fiercely male and disturbingly adult. Angela wasn't prepared for seeing him like this, all her images of him, fixed in her mind nine years ago, jarred by the unsettling reality before her now. His face looked darker, leaner, too, carved by experiences she knew nothing about, a fact that inexplicably saddened her.

The girl beside Angela pointed with her flute and said, enunciating very distinctly, "That guy is absolutely gorgeous!"

Angela remained silent. Poor Lynn didn't know the half of it, for although Jon's looks were formidable, they weren't his most attractive feature. What really drew people to him was something even more intriguing and addictive. It was his attitude; his confidence that bordered on arrogance; the effortlessness with which he succeeded at everything he tried; his energy and humor; his mercurial spontaneity. Jon was a comet whose tail people had always wanted to ride, just to feel the exhilaration.

He tossed his jacket over a seat and followed Mr. Beech onto the stage. If Angela's heart had been hammering before, it now pounded close to panic. She wasn't ready for this. How was she supposed to act? What was she supposed to say?

She and Jon had parted badly, their lifelong friendship in shambles. They'd been eighteen at the time.

No, not shambles, she amended. Shambles was what was left after a fight, but they hadn't fought. On the contrary, when they'd arrived home after that ill-fated backpacking trip, Jon had actually apologized and even tried to joke about what had happened on Mount Adams, as if it was a trivial mistake that could easily be forgotten, and his cavalier attitude had hurt. Hurt? She'd been devastated.

Then, just to grind salt into her wounds, he'd spent the remainder of that summer ignoring her. He'd blithely apologized for that, too, saying he was busy packing for college. But Angela wasn't blind. She saw the long-legged beauties he sat with on his porch. She heard their laughter as they drove off in his car. He had time, plenty of time, but apparently not for her.

And when that summer ended, he didn't even take the trouble to say goodbye in person. He'd phoned, a conversation she remembered as painfully impersonal and far too brief. And then it was over. A lifetime of friendship, over.

Sure, they'd visited each other on Christmas break; their parents expected it of them. But by then their uneasiness had grown so palpable, their conversation so strained, that Angela felt exhausted afterward. And then, that spring his parents moved to Florida, and they hadn't seen each other since. For a while they wrote, sporadic letters that eventually dwindled to sporadic postcards, but she always had the feeling they were just going through the motions of communication for the sake of politeness. And then even the postcards had stopped....

Jon paused at the footlights a few feet behind Mr. Beech, his hands in the back pockets of his jeans, drawing taut his Aran-knit sweater across his broad chest. Angela held her breath as his coal-dark, fire-bright eyes scanned the interested gathering. His talent and ambition had taken him so many exciting places that for one fleeting moment she wondered if he would even recognize her now. Not that it mattered. In fact, she hoped he wouldn't. She no more wanted to resume an acquaintance with Jon Stoddard than she wanted to enter shock therapy.

His gaze moved over the orchestra, across the first violins, through the violas and steadily on to the flutes. Suddenly his head jerked back with a jolt of recognition.

Caught in his dark stare, Angela swallowed hard and waited through an electrified few seconds. And then he smiled, that slow sensuous grin that was unmistakably Jon's.

"Ladies and gentlemen—" the conductor tapped his mottled hand on the podium "—many of you have asked me if we're going to have a guest artist at this year's Christmas concert...."

Still staring at Jon, Angela's eyes widened. Guest artist? she thought, and Jon nodded almost imperceptibly.

"Until yesterday," Mr. Beech continued, "I wasn't sure myself, finances being what they are. But tonight I can finally announce that we will indeed have a soloist. His name is Jonathan Stoddard...."

A rustle of recognition moved through the orchestra.

Jon finally released her from his gaze, and she blew out a breath she hadn't been aware of holding.

"Some of you may already know Jonathan," the conductor intoned, straightening his curved spine and warming to his subject. "He grew up right here in Winston, where even as a youngster he distinguished himself as a gifted and versatile musician, winning the Young Concert Artist award at the age of. . ."

Angela sighed. Yes, she remembered: the breezy way Jon mastered instruments, one after another, while she continued to struggle with the flute; that sickening feeling whenever he won another competition—not envy, never envy—but of his pulling inexorably away.

"Therefore, it was no surprise to anyone who knew him when he won a full-tuition scholarship to Juilliard. . . ."

Angela lowered her eyes, memories of that red-letter day assailing her without warning: the rumble of his vintage Mustang idling at his mailbox; the tinny squawk as she opened her own mailbox, only to find it empty; the fragrance of daffodils that inextricably mixed those days with painful anticipation; the toot of the horn, his grin as she'd turned, his minimal thumbs-up gesture—and then her heart exploding in joy for him.

With an effort Angela directed her thoughts away from the past and back to Mr. Beech. He was telling the others what she already knew: that Jon had spent a couple of summers studying at Tanglewood and Aspen; that he'd gone on to play with a small philharmonic in Spain and another in Brazil; that he'd recorded several albums, both classical and jazz; and that he'd recently returned from an unprecedented tour of China. Since moving to Florida, Jon's mother had kept old neighbors apprised of his accomplishments by sending press releases to the local paper.

Angela's gaze swept over him slowly, all six feet two inches of him. The distance between them had grown abysmal. But then, maybe there had been an abyss there all along. That thought caused eddies of resentment to stir deep inside her.

Why they'd been best friends was beyond her, except that fate had put their homes across the street from each other. Jon was everything she was not—extroverted, unconventional, intuitive and daring. Being so strong-willed, he had dominated the friendship and far too often coerced her into accepting his choices, adopting his interests and, alas, doing things she never would have done on her own. In retrospect, Angela sometimes wondered if he'd thought she had no mind of her own.

"Jonathan finally returned to the United States in August," Mr. Beech went on, "and soon afterward learned he'd won a coveted first-horn seat with the Boston Symphony Orchestra."

Angela's back pressed into the chair. Good Lord! Jon had landed a job with the BSO? How had that news gotten by her?

Still grappling with this impressive fact, Angela was suddenly struck by another. Jon was now working in *Boston?* He was that close to Winston?

She didn't realize she was staring at him openmouthed, until he winked back. A couple of heads turned in her direction. She covered her burning cheeks with damp palms and tried to concentrate on Mr. Beech's voice.

"When I found out Jonathan was in the area, I called to see if he could fit in a brief appearance with us. He was extremely gracious and accepted my request on the spot. And so, ladies and gentlemen, please welcome our guest soloist for this year's Christmas concert, Mr. Jonathan Stoddard."

Jon acknowledged the applause of the seated musicians with a lazy smile and a low sweeping gaze. Like a bored monarch, Angela thought resentfully.

Mr. Beech held up his hand. "Mr. Stoddard has also volunteered to sit in on the rest of the program, so if you'll add another chair..."

The remainder of the rehearsal passed in a blur. Angela was jumpy, conscious every second of Jon sitting just two rows behind her. She told herself to relax. Their friendship had ended nine years ago, and nothing was expected of her now. Still, she continued to worry. After rehearsal, they'd have to say hello—common courtesy demanded at least that much—and though the transaction wouldn't take but a minute, she dreaded it more than a root canal.

Inevitably, Mr. Beech clicked off the light on his podium. "Until next Wednesday. We have only two rehearsals left." He glared sternly. "So, be here." He stepped down and made his way to the back of the stage where Jon was packing up his horn.

They probably needed to discuss the selections Jon would be playing as guest artist, Angela thought. The next moment she felt giddy with relief. Quickly and as unobtrusively as possible, she put on her coat, gathered up her things and headed for the exit.

Outside snow was falling, muting the multicolored lights decorating Winston's main downtown street. Angela paused under the street lamp in front of the theater to dig out her keys from her purse, her legs still quivering.

The door behind her opened, and her already strung-out nerves pulled even tighter. Which was ridiculous, she told herself. It was probably just another musician eager to leave. Nevertheless, she took a hurried step off the curb.

"Hey, Westgate. Slow down."

Angela's heart stopped. No, it wasn't just another musician. Had she actually believed it would be? Suddenly she felt trapped, light-headed and almost sick to her stomach.

With cheeks ablaze, she turned and stepped back onto the sidewalk. "Hello, Jon."

He covered the distance between them in an instant, then set down his horn case and pulled her into a tight embrace. "I can't believe this!" He laughed, hugging her right off her feet. Angela was overwhelmed by a sudden onslaught of leather and wool, coarse beard and hard muscle.

"I can't believe this!" he repeated, and she wondered what was so strange about finding her playing with the WSO. Where else would she be? *She* wasn't the one who'd left town.

Finally he set her down but still held on to her shoulders. "How are you, Angel?"

Her breath caught. Angel. She'd forgotten. Jon was the only person who called her that. Angel. A name she'd always secretly loved, his own private endearment for her. But then, maybe she'd invested it with more than he'd ever intended.

She tried to remain impassive. "Very well. Yourself?"

"Great, great." He flashed her one of his ten-thousand-watt smiles, but with a flick of her long blond hair she looked away. Maybe nine years had done the trick for him, but if he thought *she* had forgotten any of his callous, self-centered and hurtful behavior, he had a big surprise coming.

At last he released her and stepped back. "Well, you're certainly looking good these days. All grown-up and polished."

"Thank you." She didn't smile. She'd always favored clothing with a polished classic look.

"Not just your clothes," he said uncannily. "It's your face, your hair. Are you doing something different with it?"

Angela thought about the three years it had taken her to grow it so long, the regular hot-oil treatments and expensive highlighting she had done at the salon. "Yes. I've taken to combing it."

Jon's smile reached his eyes. "Well, you're doing a good job."

Angela refused to be charmed. "So, Boston, huh?"

"Yeah." She heard the slow pleased grin in his voice.

"You must be very happy."

"I am."

Angela chewed on the inside of her cheek. Although the BSO was one of the most prestigious orchestras in the world, Jon probably saw it as just one more whistle-stop reference to add to his résumé.

"Where are you living?" she asked, resigned to the fact that the situation called for at least a modicum of conversation. As soon as they'd talked enough to fill the courtesy quota, she'd get in her car and drive off, forgetting that Jon Stoddard had ever been here.

"Cambridge. I'm subletting an apartment from a Harvard professor who's teaching abroad this semester." His gaze traveled the gaily lit street, over the plate-glass-and-brick facades of the small stores that looked the very same as when he and Angela had been children. His eyes narrowed with an emotion she couldn't quite peg.

"Say, is there someplace we can go for coffee?" he asked abruptly.

"C-coffee?" This wasn't supposed to happen. What was wrong with the man? Didn't he feel any of the awkwardness she was suffering? "Gosh, I'm sorry, Jon. I...I can't."

A tiny frown etched itself between his brows. "Sure. Maybe next week."

"Next week?"

"Mmm. Rehearsal?"

With a hand that shook visibly, Angela brushed snow from her eyelashes. "Jon, if there's anyone who doesn't need to come to rehearsal, it's you. I could hear you over those seventy other people."

He shrugged. "It's a good excuse to visit you again."

Angela's discomfort deepened. She didn't want Jon visiting. She knew what he was like. One day a visit, and the next your life turned into an amusement-park ride. Well, she wouldn't allow it. She liked her life exactly as it was—quiet, ordered, purposeful.

"Angel, are you sure you can't squeeze a cup of coffee into your evening?"

She fidgeted with the strap of her shoulder bag. "I have things to do."

"Half a cup?" He brought himself down to her eye level, smiling his most winsome smile.

She sighed, feeling transparent. "Well, maybe half a cup. There's a diner up the road."

She noted the disappointment in his eyes even as he said, "Sounds good."

She felt thoroughly ungracious. "Or," she added, "you could come to my place..."

"Sounds even better." Jon's smile returned in full.

Snow swirled against her scalding cheek. Now she'd done it.

"Let's go then." Jon picked up his horn case. "Where are you parked?"

"Across the street."

"Great. I'll follow you." He walked briskly to a low-slung sportscar glinting a deep blue in the streetlight.

Angela's guard fell for a moment and she gave an incredulous gasp. "This isn't yours, is it?"

"My pride and joy."

She stepped into the street and stalked the car as if it were an alien craft. "It's a Mercedes, Jon!"

"Is it really? Hot damn!"

She leaned over to admire the rich interior. "I thought we took a vow against owning Mercedes."

"That was then. Besides, why are you drooling?"

"W-why?" she stammered, realizing she had initiated this slide into familiarity. "Uh, because I have to toodle home in that thing." She pointed across the street to her sensible five-year-old Ford.

"How very like you, Westgate."

Angela bristled under his knowing tone, and she snapped, "See you in a few minutes."

As Angela drove the four miles to her condo, her foul mood deepened. "How very like you," she repeated mockingly, glaring at Jon's low headlights in her rearview mirror. Her eyes caught the reflected light and sparkled back at her, big and blue, belying the long trying day she'd put in.

Jon didn't know her any better than he knew the man in the moon. She'd changed, and the changes ran a lot deeper than outward polish. She drummed her gloved fingers on the steering wheel, then gave it a short sharp jab.

Jon had *never* known her, the big conceited jerk! One day when they were sixteen, he'd mentioned that he was writing a piano piece for her. She'd been intrigued, maybe even a little flattered—until she'd heard the stupid thing. It was a waltz. "The Angel Waltz," he'd called it.

She didn't say anything then, because at the time she didn't understand the reasons herself, but she'd hated it. With its steady one-two-three rhythm and sweet predictable melody, the piece had been a perfect emblem of their relationship. Jon had never seen her for the complex person she really was. The waltz had said it all: here was a person you didn't have to think too hard about or expect to be surprised by.

Well, Jon Stoddard would have his socks blown off if he got to know her now. But she wasn't about to give him the opportunity. Oh, no! This was going to be the fastest cup of coffee he'd ever had!

CHAPTER TWO

ANGELA FLIPPED ON her directional blinker and led Jon through the stone gate and up the lighted drive toward a hamlet of two-storied quasi-colonial row houses, one of which she now called home. Candles and Christmas trees glowed in almost every window, a sharp contrast to the darkness of her own place.

Jon parked beside her and got out of his car. Planting his hands low on his hips, he turned slowly, giving the development an assessing gaze. "Give me a break, Westgate! You really live here?"

She cocked her chin. "Lock, stock and barrel."

"But I thought we took a vow against condos."

"That was then." She marched up the path to her door, leaving him to whatever recollections he was trying to exhume. She would have none of it. What was the point?

Inside, she stamped the snow off her boots and switched on a living room lamp. "Here, let me take your jacket."

"Thanks." Jon's penetrating gaze was already roving, taking in the neat room and its traditional furnishings. "All sarcasm aside, how did you end up living here?"

"It was my mother's idea. She got tired of dealing with the old house, especially after my father died. It was unwieldy—so big, so many repairs."

"True, but it had character. All the houses in our neighborhood did."

Angela shrugged noncommittally. "Come on into the kitchen. We can talk while I put on the coffee."

"Do you miss it? The old house?"

Angela willed her face to remain blank. "This is so convenient and modern, how could I?" She opened the refrigerator and reached for the coffee.

"Well, I miss ours. My parents have a nice place now, but it's just not the same." He took the can from her, and while she filled the glass carafe with water, measured out the fragrant grind.

"I'm sorry I wasn't here for her funeral."

"I didn't expect you. You were…heaven knows where."

"I still feel bad. Your mother was a wonderful lady, and what I'm trying to say is, I'm sorry she's gone."

Angela gazed up into his dark velvet eyes and allowed a moment of honesty. "I know."

"It must be tough, with Christmas coming up."

She swallowed. "Sometimes. More than half a year has passed, but still…"

Jon tipped up her chin. "If there's anything I can do…"

Angela wished she could believe he was serious, but she couldn't. Even if he hadn't treated her so hurtfully, leaving her with a heart full of resentment, too much time had passed. They had drifted, grown apart. They weren't friends anymore, no matter what he tried to pretend.

"Let's go sit where it's more comfortable while the coffee's brewing," she suggested coolly.

He followed her into the living room. "So, what's going on in your life these days, besides playing flute for old man Beech and the Winston Symphony?"

Angela sat in one of the wing chairs and wondered how to respond to the sarcasm she thought she heard in Jon's voice. "Winston might not be the BSO, but it isn't chopped liver, either."

Jon looked slightly confused.

"I'm teaching mostly," she replied. "I split my time between the high school and Winston College."

Instead of sitting, Jon paced the room, taking in the details. "That right? College? You must have an advanced degree, then."

"Yes. In musicology."

"Ah." He brushed his long fingers across a shelf of books, then stepped back to take in the floor-to-ceiling array. "You were always such a good student." His voice was lightly mocking.

"Bet your life I was," she replied more vehemently than she'd intended. Jon didn't really know, did he? He hadn't been around to see her truly shine.

He crossed in front of the fireplace over to the entertainment center. "How did the University of New Hampshire turn out for you?" But he seemed more interested in her videotape collection than in her college career.

"It was great." Something deep inside her made her add, "It wasn't Juilliard, of course...."

Jon glanced over his shoulder, frowning again.

"Come sit," she said. "You're making me nervous."

"Oh, sorry." Before he did, though, he pressed a button on her stereo system and a soft-rock radio station came wafting through the speakers—an old Karen Carpenter song.

"I hear Beech is retiring after this concert." He sat on the camelback sofa opposite her and, resting his elbows on his knees, tapped his fingertips together, tense with nervous energy.

"Uh...yes. He suffered a mild heart attack last summer."

"That's too bad. He'll be hard to replace."

"Yes." Her pulse hammered. She considered telling Jon that she was hoping to be that replacement, but then remembered she wanted to keep him out of her life. Besides, he wouldn't understand either her drive or her ability.

"So, how do you like the place?" she asked.

"It's okay, even if it is a condo. It's solid, substantial. Has a strong sense of permanence. Or is that just because you have so much furniture from the old house?"

Angela tipped her head. "You remember?"

"Yes." For a moment she almost offered to take him on a tour, but she used her mother's room as an office now, and too much of herself was scattered about: the poster of Catherine Comet, her favorite female conductor; a score she'd already started to annotate in anticipation of the March concert. It wasn't so much that she was embarrassed over her presumption that she was going to get the directorship—the marked-up score was more a sign of her need to be prepared than of her ego—she just didn't want Jon to see it and start asking questions.

"Our coffee smells about ready." She almost launched herself from the chair, eager to escape the tension created by their thin conversation.

But even when she was alone preparing the tray, her uneasiness remained with her. She wished Jon hadn't come back, wished she'd skipped rehearsal tonight, wished she hadn't opened her big mouth and invited him over. She had the feeling she'd dragged in a lighted Roman candle and was just standing by waiting for it to go off.

"Here we are." She set the laden silver tray on the coffee table. In her absence, Jon had changed the radio station—Miles Davis replacing Karen Carpenter—and resumed wandering again.

"Do you still take one sugar?" she asked.

"Uh, no. No sugar. Who's this?"

Angela glanced up to find Jon holding a small framed photograph. The spoon slipped from her hand with a clatter. "His name's Ivan Dillane."

Jon scowled. "Yvonne?"

"Ivan. I-v-a-n," she spelled out. "But he prefers a more ethnic pronunciation. Ee-von. He teaches at the college, too."

"Ah. Is he your man of the hour?"

"And when have I ever had a man of the hour?" Loving-and-leaving had always been Jon's specialty, not hers.

"Of course. You started looking for Mr. Right when you were ten. I forgot. So, is he it? Mr. Right?"

"Could be. He's just about everything I've ever looked for in a man." She attempted a confident smile, but the afternoon's argument repeated on her.

"Hmm. I didn't realize you were into the tweedy professorial type."

"Why not?" Her mouth tightened. "We only have everything in common—our jobs, acquaintances, our sense of traditional family values, even our leisure activities. We both love to attend auctions and spend quiet nights at home."

"Hmm. How old's this guy, anyway?"

"Only thirty-two. It's the beard that makes him look older."

Jon placed the picture on the coffee table and sat on the sofa. "What does he teach?" His eyes moved from the photo to her and back again as if trying to see them as a couple.

"Russian language and literature."

"Really? Must be an interesting guy."

"Yes." She fixed her gaze on the coffee cup in her lap, searching for a way to steer Jon clear of her private life. "How about you, Jon? Are you seeing anyone these days?"

He broke into a smile. "Yes, as a matter of fact. Her name is Cynthia Gardner. We met in Bahia a year ago when she was doing a shoot for *Mademoiselle*."

"A model?"

"Yes."

Angela should have expected as much. What she didn't expect was the dull ache of disappointment she felt as the words "a year ago" sank in.

"Are you two serious?"

He took a while to answer. "We could be."

"Really?" Angela stared into the middle space between them. Jon had never been serious about anyone in his life. "How do you and Cynthia keep in touch? Being a model, she must have to live in New York."

He nodded. "When she's working she does. Then she comes home to her parents in Boston."

"Oh. How...convenient." Angela took another sip of coffee, choking on barely enough to wet her lips. Is that why he'd applied for the BSO slot? To be near Cynthia?

"W-would you like a piece of cranberry bread?" She held out the plate and noticed it was shaking. "My sister Peg made it."

"No, thanks. How is Peg these days?"

"Very well. Would you believe she's expecting her first grandchild?"

"That right?" He smiled. "Well, she did have a head start on you, being nineteen years older and all. Where's she living?"

"Vermont, up by Stowe."

Jon's eyes narrowed. "Oh, that's too bad."

"What do you mean?"

He shook his head regretfully. "I was hoping you wouldn't be alone here after your mother died."

"I'm hardly alone, Jon. Granted, Peg isn't exactly within drop-in distance, but we visit often enough. And I have Ivan and my students and the WSO. I have more companionship than I know what to do with." Feeling inexplicably uneasy, she picked up the picture of Ivan and returned it to the shelf.

She and Jon had touched on just about every topic people cover after not seeing each other for a while—family, jobs, love lives. It was time for him to leave. So, why didn't he? And why did he have that disturbing little frown between his eyes, even when he smiled?

"Well, I should be hitting the road."

Angela turned from the bookshelf, somewhat startled. There had once been a time when, young and foolish, they'd believed they could pick up each other's thoughts telepathically.

"But before I go..." He paused.

Angela felt her scalp prickle in apprehension. "What?"

"When I was looking over your shelves before, I couldn't help noticing you have the first eighteen years of our lives preserved on videotape." Jon had always been observant, but now Angela felt positively invaded.

She glanced over her shoulder at the row of neatly marked video boxes. "Yes. Even the old eight-millimeter home movies my father took. I had them transferred to tape a few years ago." Her eyes were suddenly pleading. "You can't possibly want to see them now. There must be eight hours—"

"Oh, no. Of course not." Jon sounded sincere, yet he avoided her eyes.

But Angela didn't care if he was disappointed. She didn't want to go tripping down any damn memory lane with him. Their friendship was over, gone with the warm breeze that had blown over them that summer morning when they'd awakened on Mount Adams nine years ago.

"Maybe you'll let me borrow them sometime."

"Sure." Angela remained standing, trying to give him the hint.

"Though in all honesty, I'd give my eyeteeth to see the lip-synch contest right now." He paused, flashing her one of his most convincing grins.

"You can't be serious."

"C'mon, Angel. Just our act. How long can it take? Three, maybe four minutes?"

She laughed but stood her ground. "Sorry. You'll just have to wait until you borrow it. And I have to warn you, Jon, you'll probably be disappointed. The past is always brighter in memory."

Jon frowned and stared at her. "Angel, what's the matter?"

The genuine concern in his voice unnerved her. She looked away, swallowed, then replied, "Nothing." She could feel his hot scrutiny in the silence that followed.

"Sorry," he finally said. "I guess I'm pushing too hard, aren't I?"

Angela froze, realizing they'd been on the same wavelength all along. "What do you want from me, Jon?"

"I . . . I don't know." He hauled himself off the sofa and paced the room restlessly, his hand pressed to the nape of his neck. Finally he turned to her, his casual smile back in place. "Hey . . . gotta go. I have a long drive ahead of me."

Without arguing, Angela retrieved his jacket from the closet and held it open for him.

"Thanks for the coffee." He flipped up his collar and turned to leave.

Impulsively, Angela gripped his arm. "Jon, wait. I'm sorry if this visit hasn't turned out as you expected. But, well . . ." She let his arm go and stared through the storm door at the sugary snow glistening on her front steps. "A lot of time has passed since we last saw each other. We've changed, developed individual interests, made new friends. And all that—" she wafted a hand toward the videotapes "—that was then. Not that I don't have fond memories, but, well, friends drift apart. It just happens, as naturally as childhood ends."

Jon gazed through the fogging glass. "Even best friends?"

Unexpectedly, Angela felt a clutching in her chest. "Those especially."

He only nodded, a tight gesture of resignation, before stepping out into the night.

She closed the door as soon as the engine of his Mercedes turned over, then distractedly gathered up their coffee things and put them in the kitchen. She was right. They probably didn't have a thing in common anymore, and even if they did, his insensitive treatment of her nine years ago precluded any possibility of their acting on those commonalities. Besides, she was far better off without him in her life, coercing her into foolish stunts like that lip-sync contest.

Yawning, she turned off the living room lamp, determined to put Jon from her mind and get a good night's sleep. But as she rounded the sofa, the small red eye of the VCR caught her attention. She glanced away, but it drew her back magnetically. After a moment's hesitation, she switched on the TV and in its flickering glow drew forward the hassock.

Not that she was really interested in watching this adolescent nonsense, she told herself as she slipped in a tape. Just mildly curious, that was all.

She fast-forwarded through most of the event, sponsored annually by the high school drama club, and then pressed the play button. The screen came alive at the very moment the crewnecked president of their class stood at the microphone introducing them as the Rolling Stones—Jon, herself and three of their friends.

She shook her head, still unable to believe he'd gotten her up there. The introduction was followed by applause, whistles and catcalls from the audience. Then the music started, and the student response grew thunderous.

Angela blinked, still amazed by Jon's totally uninhibited mimicking of Mick Jagger singing "Satisfaction." From the distance at which Peg had been holding the camcorder, it hardly mattered that Jon didn't look like Mick Jagger. At seventeen, he'd been tall and slim—too slim to play football, but a person never told Jon what he couldn't do—and that was enough to evoke a satisfactory resemblance. What really did the trick, though, was the sinuous way he'd gyrated across the stage. He'd been positively outrageous, and the place had gone wild.

Now the camera shifted, and Angela ducked her head. She had no interest in seeing herself pretending to be Keith Richards, no interest in being reminded that once she'd been that young and foolish.

She looked back just as the number ended. Over the applause she heard her sister's cheer—"Way to go, kids!"—and for a moment fought back a smile. On the screen, Jon dropped his stage persona and scooped a laughing seventeen-year-old Angela off her feet in an exultant twirling hug.

Quickly she fast-forwarded, over the remaining performances, over the announcement of winners and Jon's returning to the stage to claim his trophy. Of course he'd won first prize. Didn't he always?

The screen then went to fizzing static, but Angela's eyes remained fixed. A moment later the picture cleared, as she'd known it would, and suddenly it was summer. Graduation, saved for posterity on another tape, was a month behind them, college yet a month away, and she and Jon were packing his Mustang for one of their frequent trips into the White Mountains.

"And here they are, those world-famous climbers..." It was Peg's voice again, commentating in documentary style.

Angela sat on the edge of the hassock, coiled into a knot of remembrance and pain, the corners of her mouth turning ever downward. She had forgotten summer could be that golden.

"To survive the rugged terrain of New Hampshire's high country," Peg went on, "a camper must be prepared with the right equipment." Here, the camera zoomed in on Angela's sturdy boots. Then, "Do something, Angie."

To comply, Angela tucked her walking stick under her arm and did a lighthearted soft-shoe shuffle across the driveway, ending with a poke to Jon's backside as he bent over his car's engine. Jerking upright, he bumped his head on the raised hood and swore.

Angela, sitting in the dark of her living room, bit her quivering lower lip, laughed aloud and then drew in a shuddering breath. The next moment, two hot tears spilled down her cheeks.

She watched Jon join her dance, then pull her into an exaggerated tango, his thick dark curls falling in sharp contrast against her pale straight bob. She studied their open faces, looked hard into their guileless eyes and wondered if either of them had suspected that when the sun rose the next morning, they'd no longer be friends but lovers.

CHAPTER THREE

BY THREE-THIRTY, the campus was already darkening. Angela crossed the quadrangle as quickly as her leather-soled boots would allow. The snow that had been tramped to an opaque mush during the busy day was beginning to freeze in treacherous patches. She huddled into her white wool coat, wishing her day was over. Wishing, too, she wasn't so tired.

A snappy wind gusted down the open hill, rocking the tall lighted fir tree in the center of the quad and causing Angela's eyes to water. For the hundredth time that day she cursed Jon Stoddard for keeping her awake half the night. Oh, she'd tried to sleep, but hours after he'd left, the very air around her had still vibrated with his presence. She'd continued to hear the deepened timbre of his voice, see the new lines of maturity in his face, smell his spicy scent, feel his roughened cheek. In one short visit, it seemed, Jon had saturated her senses.

Well, it didn't matter now, she thought. It was over. Of course, she'd still have to face him again at possibly two more rehearsals and then at the concert, but there would be no repetition of last night's folly, no friendly chitchat or going back to her place for coffee. In fact, after the blunt send-off she'd given him, she'd be surprised if he even said hello next time they met.

"Angela!"

She recognized Ivan's voice and turned on the steps of the faculty building. He caught up with her and, removing his pipe, kissed the side of her mouth. Reflexively, she backed off, uncomfortable with public shows of affection.

"Heading upstairs?"

She nodded, ducking eagerly into the warmth of the building. "I have to get some things out of my office for my four o'clock class."

"I'll keep you company, then."

They climbed the stairs to the second floor where Angela unlocked the door to a space that could justifiably be called a cubicle. Ivan closed the door behind her, and the room seemed to shrink even more. He wasn't a particularly tall man, but he was broad and solid.

He unbuttoned his coat, then removed his karakul hat, lifting carefully from the crown and setting it on Angela's desk. His fine sandy hair crackled with static electricity.

With a small shrug of apology, Angela transferred his hat to a chair and opened her briefcase. "What are you doing for dinner tonight?" She smiled warmly, hoping to ease any lingering tension from the previous day's argument.

He tapped his pipe into an ashtray, kept on a windowsill just for him. "Not a helluva lot. I have a department meeting at five. We're sending out for pizza."

"Oh, that's too bad. I was hoping we could get together. Ah, well. Maybe tomorrow night."

"Yes, of course."

"What? Oh, that's right." They always ate together on Fridays. Chinese takeout and a rented movie. Her place. The routine never varied.

"Excuse me, Ivan." She brushed past him to get to her record cabinet.

"Why didn't you call me last night? You always call after rehearsal."

Angela's stomach muscles bunched. She selected an album and fitted it into her briefcase. The plain truth was she'd forgotten to call. After Jon had left, she'd been so upset she'd simply forgotten.

"Sorry. I really am. But..." She contemplated telling Ivan about Jon's visit, but instinct told her to keep the two men apart even though logic failed to come up with a reason. "I was so bushed I went straight to bed."

"Angela, Angela." Ivan sighed as if she were a child who constantly tried his patience. "You know how worried I get when you're out at night by yourself. Call me next time, all right?"

Angela nodded, opened a drawer and frisked the files within for the handouts she needed to copy.

"All right?" he asked more forcefully.

Her fingers stilled. Ivan's protectiveness toward her was one of his most endearing qualities, but the undertone in his voice now unsettled her. "Yes, I'll call." She shut her brief-case, glanced at her watch and headed for the door.

But on the way Ivan gripped her arm. "About yesterday..." The bunched muscles in her stomach knotted. "I was wondering, have you been thinking about what I said?"

"Yes. I told you I would." She tried to pull away, but he tightened his hold.

"I'm serious this time. We've been together too long, we're both adults, and these are the nineties. No one would condemn us or be surprised if we... loosened the reins on our relationship a bit. As it exists now, it *is* sort of Victorian, don't you agree? In fact, most people would be surprised if they knew just how chaste it's been."

Angela rubbed a spot between her brows where a head-ache was starting. "I said I'd think about it. And you agreed to give me until Sunday."

He let her go, nodding. "It just seems a thing one shouldn't have to think about. It's a romantic relationship, for heaven's sake, not a military strategy. If you really cared about me, you wouldn't have to think at all. We'd just be sleeping together, and I can't help wondering if something else isn't wrong, something you haven't told me."

Angela reared back, her cheeks warming. "Like what?"

"Well, like sexual dysfunction."

Her eyes snapped wide open.

"It's nothing to be embarrassed about. We could go to therapy together."

"Thank you. That's just what I needed to hear. Dysfunction." She took a determined step toward the door, only to have her path blocked.

"Well, how do you explain it? There isn't a couple we know who isn't ... intimate."

"Really? And how have you verified such a fact, Ivan?"

"Now don't get testy. I'm only trying to help."

Angela took a deep breath. Then another. "I know, I know. And maybe we ... I do have a problem. I'll give the possibility my undivided attention as soon as I can, honestly, but right now I have a class to prepare for."

She started for the door again, but suddenly Ivan pulled her against him and kissed her, hard. Angela went stiff with instinctive resistance—which he probably took as proof of dysfunction, she thought miserably. With a concerted effort, she willed herself to relax. She didn't want to hurt or upset him any more than she already had. He was too nice a person, and although relations between them were somewhat strained at present, they'd been good in the past and, no doubt, would be good again in the future.

After what seemed an eternity, he lifted his head and smiled. "Now we're making progress." When he bent to kiss her again, however, she pushed away.

"Really, I have work to do."

He moved in, anyway, encircling her in an embrace that felt more like a death lock.

"Ivan! Stop it!" Her unease became anger.

A sudden hard rap on the door made them both jump. Off guard for the moment, Ivan relaxed his hold and she was able to pull free. With a hasty pass at her hair, she swung open the door. She expected to find another teacher or a student on the other side. The last person she expected to see was Jon.

"Hello, Angel," he said evenly, but his eyes narrowed and fixed directly on Ivan.

She finally found her voice. "W-what are you doing here?"

Immediately Ivan's hand curled into her shoulder. "Who's he?" he demanded.

"Who are you?" Jon volleyed back.

Angela gulped. "Seems introductions are in order. Jon, this is my friend, Ivan Dillane. Ivan, this is Jon Stoddard, the guest soloist for this year's WSO Christmas concert."

She wondered if she could leave explanations at that, but from the scowling puzzlement in Ivan's gray eyes, she knew she couldn't. Why would the guest soloist be meeting her here? "Jon also happens to be—" she gulped again "—an old friend. He's just recently returned to the States after several years abroad."

The men sized each other up before shaking hands.

"I hope I'm not interrupting anything," Jon said.

Angela got the distinct impression he knew exactly what he was interrupting.

"I just thought I'd drive up for a visit."

She wanted to remind him he'd visited only last night, but then realized that would catch her out in her fib about going to bed early. "Well, how nice. We barely had a chance to talk last evening."

Jon glanced from her to Ivan. "Yes." He took her briefcase from her and, gripping her arm, made to escort her out of her office. "You were heading somewhere, right?"

"Uh . . . yes. The photocopy machine downstairs." From the corner of her eye she saw Ivan puff up with anger.

"A pity you came at such an inconvenient time, Mr. Stoddard. Angela has a class at four."

"Oh, does she?" Jon's expression brightened. "And what about you, Ivan? Do you have a class, too?"

Gripping Angela's other arm, Ivan replied, "No, I'm done for the day."

She eyed him curiously. "Except for your four o'clock tutorial, and it appears he's eager to get an early start. Hello, Kevin."

A rangy young man, sitting halfway up the stairs to the third floor, smiled at Angela and blushed.

"Ah, then this is where we say goodbye. It was a pleasure meeting you, Ivan," Jon said, dismissing him with infuriating congeniality.

"Ee-von."

"What?"

"You called me Eye-vin just now."

"I did? Oh, I'm so sorry."

Ivan hitched his shoulders, once, twice. "I'll call you later, Angela," he said. "Better yet, I'll stop by. My meeting should be done by seven, and you'll already be home. Right?" He glanced at Jon, his eyes sharp with challenge.

"Yes, of course."

"So long," Jon called amiably, as Ivan stamped up the stairs to his office. When he got no reply, he chuckled. "Cheerful fellow, your Yvette."

For a moment, Angela's guard fell and she grinned. Immediately she was sorry. They weren't fifteen anymore. The days when they could poke fun at each other's love interests were long gone.

"You shouldn't have done that," she snapped, tromping down the stairs.

"Done what?" Jon grinned rakishly.

"Made fun of him. Ivan isn't just some guy I'm hoping'll ask me to the prom. I happen to care about him. A lot." She received a careless shrug in response.

They entered the brightly lit workroom, and Angela headed straight for the photocopy machine in a flurry of busyness. She positioned a handout on the machine, closed the cover, pressed thirty copies and then the print button.

"So—" She faced Jon squarely "—what are you doing here?"

He leaned against the worktable, arms folded across his supple leather jacket, one booted ankle crossed over the other. Angela noticed a secretary on the far side of the room peeking at him with badly concealed interest. As upset as Angela was, she couldn't blame the woman. Jon was big and bad and beautiful, and she could barely keep from staring at him herself.

"I don't suppose you'd believe I missed you?" he drawled.

"Not a chance."

"Okay, how's this? I've picked up with a jazz band in Cambridge, and I was wondering if you'd like to come hear us play Sunday night."

Angela fixed her gaze on the bright seam of light oozing from the covered machine. "A *jazz* band?" she echoed.

"Yeah. I've always played jazz on the side. You know that."

She snatched up the fresh copies from the tray and tapped them into order as if trying to knock some sense into them.

"It's a great group of guys, and I like the place. It's small, intimate."

She opened her briefcase and tossed in the handouts, wondering why she was getting so riled. Jon wasn't her concern. She had her own affairs to tend to. "What do you play with this jazz band?"

"Piano. Just like the old days."

Angela shook back her long blond hair as if shaking off the phrase "old days." She said cooly, "I don't play that sort of stuff anymore myself. My schedule's too busy, and one would think yours is even busier."

Jon chuckled dryly. "You don't know the half of it."

"So, what are you trying to do to your career, Jon?" She slapped another sheet into the machine and lowered the cover.

"What's that supposed to mean?"

"It means you've just landed one of the best jobs on the planet, and instead of concentrating on it, you're diffusing your energy, losing focus."

"Huh?"

"Oh, I know, you never could sit still. But, Jon, this is it. Real life. Isn't it time you got serious?"

Jon's jaw hardened. "There was a time when a thought like that wouldn't have even crossed your mind, let alone your lips. What's happened to you, kid?"

Angela placed the stack of still-warm copies into her briefcase and snapped it shut. "Maybe I've just grown up."

His face dropped. "Thanks a million, pal."

Angela glanced aside, realizing she was vastly overreacting, and the worst part was she didn't even understand why. Perhaps it was merely a response to his showing up so unexpectedly.

"Jon, if all you wanted to do was invite me to Cambridge, you could've done that by phone. Why are you really here?"

With a glance toward the eavesdropping secretary, Jon picked up Angela's briefcase and ushered her out to the corridor.

"As briefly as I can put it, I've missed our friendship, Angel, and now that I've returned to the area, I want it back."

Angela shrugged out of his grip. "Just like that. You want it back."

"Yes."

"Just like..." She snapped her fingers.

"Yes. It isn't a complicated concept, sweetheart. I don't know why you're having such trouble with it."

"Don't be cute."

"I can't help it."

Angela pressed her fingers over her eyes and groaned. "I thought I made it clear to you last night—"

"The only thing that's clear, my friend, is that unlike you, I don't know how to turn off eighteen years of memories.

You're woven too close into the fabric of my life. How do you do it, Angel? I'd really like to know."

Angela squirmed under the intensity of his stare. "If that's so, why didn't you contact me sooner? It's December, Jon. You returned in August."

"As I said, I've been busy. Do you have any idea what it's like being thrust into the full working schedule of the BSO, five, sometimes six performances a week, the program changing constantly?"

"But you still had time for Cynthia and a jazz band." Angela hated herself immediately. She sounded so peevish.

"If you really want to know, I was afraid to call you."

Angela laughed derisively. "You? Afraid?"

"Yes. I had a feeling this would be the reception I'd get."

She didn't know how to respond. Should she say she was sorry? She couldn't, not after what she'd suffered. Finally she just answered, "I have a class."

"May I sit in?"

"No!" What was wrong with the man?

"Why not?"

"Oh, I don't know. I'd just rather you didn't."

"Come on. I won't throw spitballs or pass notes."

Angela was beginning to feel trapped, and from that feeling sprang honesty. "But I won't be able to think with you there. I'll be awful."

Jon laughed, wrapped his arm around her shoulder and tugged her to his side. "No, you won't. You'll be great." And that, because he said so, was the end of the argument.

He sat in the last row, as he always had. Murderers' row, she remembered one harried teacher calling it. Students trickling in eyed him with interest, but Jon remained cool, his long legs stretched into the aisle, arms crossed over his chest and a hellish glint sparkling in his midnight eyes. Standing at the podium, Angela felt those eyes running an amused survey of her. She must look very staid to him, she thought, in her neat boiled-wool jacket and matching beige skirt, with simple gold studs adorning her ears and oh-so-sensible low-heeled boots protecting her feet.

The hands of the clock reached the hour, and her heart lodged in her throat. Damn him! she swore silently. This was her life, not a joke. She scanned the class, gathered up her dignity and began.

As usual, she was well prepared and somehow muddled through. But when her lecture came up fifteen minutes short, she decided to make Jon pay for causing her to talk so fast. She apologized to the class for hurrying—as if she'd planned it that way all along—but, she said, she wanted to introduce them to a special guest.

In the back row, Jon sat up as if he'd been poked.

When she explained what Jon did for a living, interest ignited immediately. "If you have any questions, I'm sure Mr. Stoddard will be happy to answer them."

A dozen hands went up. They asked about his background, who his favorite composers were, how often he practiced, even what he earned. They were still asking questions when the period ended.

Jon ambled up the aisle once the last of the students was gone. "Good save, Teach."

Angela turned her back to him to erase the board. If anyone had saved the day, it was Jon. He'd fielded the unexpected questions with such easy grace and humor.

"So, where's a good place to eat around here?" he asked.

She eyed him over her shoulder. "What?"

"Do you have a favorite restaurant?" He slapped his forehead. "Oh. That's the other reason I drove up here—to take you to dinner."

She wasn't amused. "Jon, all I want to do is get home, climb into my fuzzy bathrobe and..."

"That's okay, too. We can pick up a couple of hamburgers on the way."

With a soulful sigh, she slipped on her coat. "You aren't going to quit, are you?"

He shook his head fractionally, his firm sensuous mouth curled at one corner.

She huffed. "All right. We'll have dinner, but here, on campus."

"Here?"

"Yes." She didn't want to go off to any restaurant where conversation might grow too personal, and she certainly didn't want him back at her place. "It's...faster."

"Oh, yeah. I forgot. Yvette will be at your place by seven." He zipped his jacket and flipped up the collar. "Bundle up, Teach. It's cold out there."

"I know how to dress, and you'd better stop calling Ivan..." Jon looped her scarf around her neck and mouth twice, so that the rest of her words came out woolly.

"I've always wanted to do that."

"Wha?"

"Gag a teacher."

All Angela could do was glare.

Outside, evening had nearly fallen, a quarter moon gleaming silver in an indigo sky.

"This is a nice little school," Jon commented.

"Hmm." Angela scanned the neoclassic buildings, their white pediments pale in the moonlight. Christmas candles glowed from every multipaned window. "It's what you expect of a New England college. Brick and ivy and maple-lined paths."

"Are you happy here, Angel?"

"Sure, I'm happy," she answered automatically.

"Then...everything is good with you?"

She looked at him askance. "Yes. My life is very full, very rewarding."

He nodded, that disturbing little frown between his eyes again. "So, what do you teach, besides music appreciation?"

"Here? That's it. But I also direct the chorus. And over at the high school I have two classes in theory and, of course, my string orchestra."

Jon's steps slowed significantly. "You conduct?"

She turned on the icy path to face him. "Yeah, I conduct."

A slow smile lit his face. "Well, I'll be damned."

"You probably will be."

He laughed, scratching his head. "When the hell did you decide—"

"Junior year of college." They resumed walking. "And you don't have to look so astonished."

"Sorry. It just takes a little getting used to. You were always so quiet."

"Quiet doesn't mean timid, Jon."

"I'm surprised you're not interested in Mr. Beech's job."

"Who says I'm not interested?" Too late she realized the admission was out. She waited, feeling her cheeks grow warmer by the second.

When Jon failed to respond, she glanced over. He was staring straight ahead, his expression unreadable. *He doesn't believe I'm qualified,* she thought. *He's thinking I've become an overreaching fool.*

She wanted desperately to change the subject. "Let's take this path," she suggested. "It's quicker."

"To what? Are we still on our way to dinner?"

"Oh, yes."

They walked on, their breath billowing in white clouds over their heads.

"This is so strange," Jon said after a while.

"What is?"

"Being here like this, walking with you to dinner."

"I don't follow."

"Well . . . I can't help thinking that this is what college might've been like if we'd gone to the same school." His voice was thick and wistful.

"Oh."

"That was when the thread got broken, wasn't it, Angel? When we went off to school."

She tensed. "It couldn't be helped. It's where we applied, where we got scholarships..."

"I know. But I still feel I missed out on something. We stopped sharing things. There's a gap..."

"Well, you needn't beat me up with the fact. It wasn't *my* fault." Immediately she wished she'd kept the thought to herself. The air between them crackled with remembrance and recrimination.

"Where exactly are you taking us to dine?" Jon's question was an obvious digression, one she gladly embraced.

"The cafeteria."

"Oh, joy."

"I don't exactly relish the idea myself, but as I said, it's fast." And safe, she added to herself.

They entered the dining hall and were immediately hit with a wall of music pulsing from the jukebox. Silver and gold garlands hung in haphazard loops from the ceiling, while cardboard Santas and snowmen smiled from support columns. Angela gazed over the noisy sea of young people, took a moment to question her sanity, then plunged forward to the food line.

"Mm-mm. Tonight's special smells like greasy french fries and burnt coffee. Can't wait!" Jon's words caught in her hair, puffs of warm breath that sent shivers down her back. She pressed forward, needing to put more distance between them.

They finally purchased their meals and found space at a table. Four guys who looked like basketball players sat on either side of them. As she'd anticipated, it was difficult to talk, and so they ate, Jon looking increasingly frustrated.

"Tell me more about your Yvette," he said, leaning in. "How long've you two been together?" Apparently he was going to make a stab at conversation, anyway.

"Half a year, and stop calling him Yvette."

Jon's smirk told her he'd do whatever he wanted. "He surprises me. I thought he'd be proper and reserved."

"He is," Angela said.

"Yes, but he's rather a jealous sort, too, isn't he?"

Angela's lips tightened. "Don't be ridiculous." She glanced away uneasily. "And what if he is? I find jealousy flattering."

"I find it suffocating, a sure sign of insecurity."

"Insecurity? Ivan is the strongest person I know."

"I'm not talking biceps."

In an unguarded moment, Angela wondered what would happen if she flung a forkful of fries into Jon's know-it-all face. "Ivan is solid, mature, serious—"

"Hmm. He *is* serious, isn't he?" Jon rolled his eyes.

"Yes, he is," she returned proudly. "And he's ready to settle down. Eager to settle down. I like that in a guy."

"And you don't see his eagerness as a facet of his insecurity?"

"No! I see it as a strength. He knows what he wants. A home. A family. And I find that refreshing. I've had it up to here with guys who can't commit."

Jon pushed aside his half-eaten meal. "Are you done?"

For a moment she wasn't sure what he was referring to—her tirade against footloose egoists like himself or her meal. Her ears grew hot.

"Do you want any more of that?" he said.

"Oh. No, I'm done."

"Then let's get out of here." He scraped back his chair and stood. Angela's gaze traveled up the length of him. The differences between Jon and the boys who shared their table were remarkable, and again she was reminded of their lost years, the years that had wrought those differences.

She refused to get misty about them, though. Jon seemed to want her to, but she simply wouldn't. Those years had also been a time of confusion and pain, and she wasn't about to forget that he had been the cause. In fact, she'd had about all she could stand of Jon Stoddard for one night. He'd gotten around her attempts to send him packing two hours ago, but she wouldn't allow him to dictate any more of the evening.

Out on the sidewalk she set down her briefcase to tug on her gloves. "Well, Jon," she said in an unmistakably dismissive tone, "this has been nice." Dismissive, insincere and condescending. And she wanted him to hear it.

He didn't, or if he did, he chose to ignore it. "Let me walk you to wherever you're going."

"That's not necessary."

"I know. I'll walk you, anyway," he replied.

Frustrated and feeling somewhat disoriented, Angela headed toward the faculty building. She hadn't a thing to do there, but she'd concoct some excuse once they arrived.

They walked on, the crunch of their boots in the snow amplified by the silence of the night.

"Angel, I have to be honest..."

She tensed. She knew that tone, that presage to something too personal to bear.

"The real reason I drove up here today... I simply felt I had to. I felt compelled to finally apologize and try to explain."

Angela's heart raced. She felt it thumping against the weight of her coat. "I don't know what you're talking about."

"I think you do. This tension between us—I'd hoped time would cure it and we could just sweep the whole matter under the rug, but I guess it's bigger than I thought."

Angela spun on him. "Oh, you finally figured that out, huh? How insightful! How intelligent!" Immediately, she regretted her outburst. It was an obvious admission of her vulnerability. "What do you want from me?"

He resumed a slow pace up the walk. "As I said, I feel the need to apologize. I want us to be friends again, but I can see that's not going to happen until we get over the hurdle of that... that incident."

"I don't want to talk about it."

"Angel, it's been nine years, and it's still eating away at you. Me, too. We have no choice but to talk."

Angela gazed at the faculty building across campus, wishing she was there, safely cloistered from this nightmare. "Maybe you're overestimating its importance and the effect it had on me." She hoped she sounded more cavalier than she felt.

Jon turned her to face him. "Look at me, Angel, and if you can repeat what you just said, maybe I'll believe you." Framed by the upturned collar of his leather jacket, his face was intent, very male and far too handsome. In his dark eyes shimmered the heat of that fateful July day, every nuance of sensuality she'd learned in his arms. And though the temperature now was somewhere in the bracing twenties, Angela felt a flame curl through the pit of her stomach.

Slowly, the corner of his mouth lifted in a small sad smile. "Aw, Angel, I wish I could make you understand how truly sorry I am for what happened."

She ducked her head, her eyes stinging. "Do you know what hurt most, Jon? Not talking afterward. All those days, those weeks, when you ignored me."

Jon thrust a gloved hand through his hair. "And do you realize how scared I was, Angel?"

"Scared?"

"That's right. I kept thinking, 'What've I done to our friendship? What the hell have I done?' I mean, you and I had shared all kinds of experiences, but that one..." He glanced away, eyes narrowed as if in remembered pain. "That one was a bit too complicated for most people to handle, let alone a teenage boy. If I shunned you, it wasn't because I meant to hurt you. I just didn't know what else to do."

The moisture pooling in her eyes threatened to spill. She'd always known he hadn't wanted *it* to happen and didn't understand why his saying so now should hurt this much.

"Is that the only reason?"

"Yes." He raised his right hand. "Scout's honor."

"You were never a Scout, Jon." She pulled a shredded tissue from her pocket and dabbed her nose.

"Hey, what did *you* think was going on?"

Angela looked aside. How could she even begin to tell him? "Nothing. Nothing, honestly."

They walked on in uneasy silence.

Jon finally muttered, "To this day I still don't know why we did it."

"No mystery there. Too much was happening in our lives at the time, too much change. Everything familiar and secure was coming to an end, so we turned to each other, as if clinging could hold the future at bay."

Jon nodded circumspectly. "I suppose you're right. Damn, but you always could analyze the hell out of everything and come up with some theory. Me, I seem to recall the incident growing directly out of a conversation we were having about your virginity and how embarrassed you were going off to college without any sexual experience."

"Jon, please!" Her voice leapt in panic. "I'd rather drop this discussion if you don't mind."

"But if we don't talk, I don't see how we can get back to being friends."

"Who says I *want* to get back?" Angela stopped and squinched her eyes tight. "I didn't mean for that to come out quite as coldly as it did. It's just that you and I . . . we're different now, we're adults, and it's hard for a woman who's practically engaged to one man to carry on a friendship with another. Not only hard, it's not right. It compromises the relationship she has with her fiancé."

A frown worked its way over Jon's brow. "Oh. I guess I never thought of it in that light."

"Well, do. It's important."

"You're engaged?"

"Well . . . practically."

"Hmm." He walked on pensively. "About that incident, though . . ."

"Enough about the incident."

"But we haven't solved a damn thing!"

"So what?" Angela was startled when she actually stamped her foot. They'd reached the faculty building, and in the light thrown from the door, she clearly saw amusement in Jon's face.

"That a new dance step?"

"Yes. Want to see another?" She contemplated kicking him in the shins, but took a deep calming breath, instead. "Listen, Jon, I appreciate your intentions, and it was nice having dinner with you, but, well, this just isn't going to work. Nobody's fault. I'm simply not interested in complicating my life right now, and if nothing else, you're definitely a complication." She peeked up, wondering if he was finally getting the message.

Jon's gaze swept over her so slowly her stomach fluttered. "I understand."

"You do?"

"Sure. You're still in shock, my appearing out of the blue and all. I'll give you a few days, then we'll talk again." He grinned.

"Will you never give up?" she wailed, but it was becoming increasingly difficult to restrain her amusement. They were both laughing when the door of the faculty building opened and Ivan stepped out.

"Ivan. Hi," she said awkwardly. "Done with your meeting?"

He descended the steps with slow deliberation, his gaze sliding from her to Jon and then back to her again. "I thought you were going home."

"Yes, well..."

"I'm afraid I shanghaied her into going to dinner with me, Ivan." Jon pronounced Ivan's name correctly this time. "My fault entirely."

Angela wished Ivan would say something to ease the tension he was creating. She was sure it was inadvertent and he wasn't really as upset as he appeared.

"I'm glad we've run into each other again," Jon continued. "I mentioned to Angela that I'm playing with a jazz group in Cambridge on Sunday night, but of course she wouldn't commit you to a date without checking with you first."

Angela glanced at Jon quickly, wondering why he was bringing that up again. She'd already told him no. But even more perplexing, she wished she could divine the reason he'd just called her "Angela" and why it felt so much like protection.

"Sunday night is rather inconvenient," Ivan grumbled. "We both have work the next day."

"I realize that, but it's the only night I play. And we do start early, so you can leave early."

"It's a long drive."

"True. A little over an hour. But it would be a great opportunity for us to get to know each other. You and Angela, me and Cynthia." Jon paused, and Angela was sure he was waiting for the names to take hold.

They did. Ivan relaxed noticeably. "Are you married, Mr. Stoddard?"

"No. Not yet." But his tone left the possibility open. "About Sunday, the decision is yours, but personally I hope you'll come. We can have dinner—you'll be my guests, of course. We can sit and relax, get to know one another—kind of like a double date."

Angela finally realized what Jon was up to. If it was impossible for them to be friends as individuals, then he'd arrange for them to be friends as couples.

Ivan thought for a moment. "What do you say, Angela? It might be fun."

She shouldn't have been surprised. Ivan was scrupulously careful with his money, and she'd seen the glint enter his eyes as soon as Jon mentioned the prospect of a free meal. "The idea has possibilities." She tried to sound cheerfully polite yet noncommittal.

"What time should we meet you?" Apparently Ivan mistook her answer for a yes.

"Six would be good, and it'll be easier if you go directly to the club." Jon proceeded to give directions. When he was done, he held out his hand. "Looking forward to it, Ivan."

Ivan hesitated, then shook his hand.

Angela looked away, gnawing on the inside of her cheek. The more determined she was to keep Jon out of her life, the deeper he wormed his way in. And now she was locked into a whole social evening with him. Dinner, their dates, the works.

She glared as he walked off toward the parking lot. So, Jon wanted them to become friends as couples, did he? Well, fine! She'd give him a couple, the most perfectly united couple he'd ever met. Then he'd realize that friendship with her was out of the question and relinquish this impossible pursuit.

CHAPTER FOUR

ANGELA'S SLIP slid down her body with a silky sigh. She straightened the straps and, taking a seat at her vanity, rehearsed yet again what she planned to say to Ivan when he arrived to pick her up for their evening in Boston.

"Thank you for being so patient and understanding." She shook a bottle of translucent foundation. "I've given the matter of our living together careful thought, and the first thing I want to say is, all this reflection has made me realize how special you are to me and how much I enjoy your company."

Angela set down the bottle and groaned. She hated all this tap dancing. She wished she could be blunt and simply say, "Ivan, I don't want you to move in right now. Maybe sometime in the future, but not now." But she couldn't say that, because that was the same answer she'd been giving him for ages, when what he wanted was a definitive yes or no. No quibbling. No putting off decisions until later. Yes or no. And she suspected that unless she could find a few miracle phrases to plead her case, their relationship would suffer an early demise.

She finished applying her makeup and gave her reflection a hard objective look. She was taking special care with her appearance today, fussing with makeup and hot rollers. She was even planning to wear the dress Ivan liked best on her, the pearl gray knit with dolman sleeves. It was simple and classic, yet fell over her slender figure with soft sensuality. She hoped it helped.

But it probably wouldn't. A no didn't become a yes just because you wore a nice dress when you said it, and before the night was out, Ivan would undoubtedly be talking "dysfunction" again.

She combed unsteady fingers through her hair, fluffing out the waves. If only he had the patience to wait, she was sure everything would change in a few weeks. The holidays would be over, the WSO directorship would be settled, and her mind would be much more at ease.

A frown troubled the clear deep sapphire of her eyes. She'd had a lot on her mind that day on Mount Adams, too, and hadn't been bothered by dysfunction then.

Unexpectedly, a hot shudder raced through her, and her eyes drifted closed. How easy everything had been with Jon, how natural and joyous. Nothing she'd ever done, before or since, had ever been so spontaneous or, well, so easy....

They'd spent that hot July day hiking up some fairly rigorous new trails, had pitched camp, cooked their evening meal and cleaned their utensils. Angela was tired, yet she felt an unusually deep sense of well-being, the sort that comes from facing a hard challenge and meeting it. They were camped in an area with a particularly good view, and as the sun arced toward the horizon, she and Jon lay back to watch the fiery spectacle.

In that blissful state of well-being, their conversation ebbed and flowed with a comfortable languor, while before them, a dreamlike panorama of ridges and ravines swam in the gold of the westering sun. The air was fragrant with spruce and lay about them very still, as still as the peace that had settled in Angela's heart.

Inevitably, however, their conversation meandered into the subject that was on their minds almost constantly those days—college and leaving home and all the new experiences that awaited them. Jon, as usual, was eager to get started, but for Angela life seemed to be spinning increasingly out of control. Not only had her father passed away that year, but now Jon's parents were talking about moving, and the peace she'd been enjoying deteriorated into melancholy.

Angela didn't want anything to change. She wanted this golden time with Jon to go on forever. She didn't need new experiences. Everything she needed was right here....

In the nine years that had passed since, Angela had never quite figured out how they'd drifted onto the topic of sex. At the time, though, it seemed all one seamless conversation. Angela did know that at eighteen, not only was she filled with curiosity about the subject, she was also plagued by ignorance and self-doubt.

She'd never had the nerve to ask her mother the questions she asked Jon that evening. She suspected her prim, sixty-seven-year-old mother would have fainted dead away. She wasn't that close to her sister, either, also because of an unusual age gap.

But Jon was wonderful—patient, understanding, almost paternal in his concern. She became so caught up in his deep reassuring voice that when the sun finally set, she didn't even care that she'd missed it.

Yet doubts continued to plague her. Without experience, she found sexuality such a mystery, so remote, so easy to bungle. And that, she supposed, was what led to the startling moment when Jon's eyes lighted with a warmth she'd never noticed before and he murmured, "Come here, Angel." He braced himself up on one arm, lifted the other to her and whispered, "Come here...."

Angela snapped open her eyes and found her reflection in the mirror flushed to a hectic pink. She breathed out a shaky sigh and pressed a hand to her forehead. That night, high above the world, Jon had led her into paradise. In that vast wild Eden it had all been so easy, so spontaneous—like leaping off that mountainside and gliding, wings outstretched, through the pink-and-gold clouds.

They spent that entire night together in the close privacy of Jon's tent, lost in a glorious cycle of making love and drifting into sleep, only to awake a short time later to find the fires of their passion burning higher than before. Nothing had prepared Angela for the need Jon awakened in her that night or for the euphoria she felt afterward, lying in his arms. In retrospect, she recognized it as the single most important experience of her life, and even now, after nine long years, details were so vividly etched in her sense memory that all she had to do was close her eyes to be there again, to feel the soft flannel of Jon's sleeping bag against her legs, to hear the crickets and night birds, to taste the salt of Jon's skin—and remember how deeply in love she once had been.

Angela spun away from the vanity and snatched her dress off the bed. Yes, though it angered her to admit it, she'd been in love with Jon. For her, the emotion had been growing all their lives, and what happened that night had merely been the next natural step in its growth. And she'd thought Jon felt the same. She'd thought they were poised at the start of a romance that would last them the rest of their lives. From the way he'd held her, from the urgency in his voice as he'd murmured her name, what else was she supposed to think?

But apparently she'd interpreted Jon all wrong. The next morning he was uncharacteristically reticent, and after breakfast he suggested they break camp and return home, even though they'd originally planned to stay two more days. Angela's heart splintered. After what they'd shared, she'd thought he would want to stay in the mountains with her forever. But Jon didn't care to stay even one more day. He drove them home, barely speaking, a hard unreadable expression sealing off whatever was on his mind.

Only when they were unloading her gear from his car did he finally broach the subject, which now lay between them like a huge painful burr. "Well, we've done a lot of camping together, my friend." He laughed, somewhat incredulous. "But this trip's been something else." He barely looked at her. Are you okay?"

By then, Angela could taste the tears burning in her throat. "Yes, I'm fine."

"Good. I guess I really wasn't up for camping this time. I hope you don't mind." He already had one foot in the car.

"No, I don't mind."

"Okay, well, I'll call you later, okay? Maybe we can go out for a pizza or something."

"Sure." But even then, Angela knew he was going to break his promise. No sooner did she step inside the house than she felt the first clutches of nausea. She ran to the up-stairs bathroom, dropped to her knees and was violently sick to her stomach.

"Angela dear, are you all right?" her mother called with typical alarm.

"Uh ... I think I've picked up a stomach virus."

"Goodness. Is that why you came home early?"

"Yes." Angela leapt at the ready excuse and had never been sorry since. Her paleness, her keeping to her room for the next two days didn't raise a single suspicion.

When she finally did emerge, it was to find her deepest fears confirmed. Her lifelong friendship with Jon was over.

Angela's thoughts shifted to Jon's visit to Winston College three days ago, to his claiming that he'd been frightened and confused after they'd made love. He'd blamed his behavior on his youth, but Angela knew there was more to it than that. He didn't mind having her as a friend—but as a lover, a mate? No chance. Angela Westgate wasn't smart enough, wasn't pretty or talented or interesting enough. Jon was holding out for nothing short of perfection. And in the meantime, he had places to go, things to do, and nobody was going to weigh him down. How many times had he told her that himself?

Only trouble was, Angela had thought she might be special. His relationship with her had always been so different, so honest and deep, compared to his relationships with other girls. But apparently, once they'd made love, she'd fallen from that special place and become just one more boring conquest, and worse, another potential anchor, tying him to Winston and threatening to bog down his career. Their lovemaking had meant nothing. A kindness, a lesson, nothing more.

With a ragged sigh, Angela stepped into her gray pumps. More than a year had passed before she'd felt even remotely whole again. Stupid, ugly, insignificant—that was how she'd seen herself after Jon's rejection. Eventually, though, she'd healed, music being her salvation, and after she'd discovered her passion for conducting, she'd positively flowered.

Jon was now quite definitely a thing of the past, and tonight when they met at his jazz club, she wanted him to get that message. She didn't need to be his sidekick anymore in order to have a meaningful life. She was perfectly content all by herself. Moreover, she didn't *want* to be his sidekick. Their lives glided along on very different orbits, and hers, while slower and dimmer than his, suited her just fine.

He'd gone off to chase a dream, and she was happy he was living it. But he had to realize she had dreams of her own. She'd finally found herself, found her passion, her confidence, her niche in the world. Along the way she'd also found a man who treasured her. She wasn't about to give any of that up.

IVAN KNOCKED on her door wearing his best suit and an unusually bright smile. Angela felt terrible. He was in wonderful spirits undoubtedly because he assumed she was finally going to invite him to move in with her.

She hoped he'd put off the discussion until later, after they'd survived their night out with Jon and Cynthia. She so wanted to present a united happy front in their company. But no sooner did they swing onto the highway than Ivan lowered the boom and asked if she had reached a decision. With a voice that wavered noticeably, Angela recited her practiced lines. Her heart was thumping.

"Fine," he said coldly. She glanced across the front seat to a profile set in stone. "Fine."

"You don't mind waiting, then?"

"Do I have a choice?" He was granting her a reprieve, which was what she wanted, but he wasn't going to be happy about it. She sank into her seat, wondering if he planned to sulk the rest of the night. Oh, Lord, oh, Lord, she worried. This wouldn't do.

The city of Boston came at them in a dazzle of lights, speed and heightened energy. Jon's world, Angela thought almost resentfully, a world where, as often as she'd visited, she still felt slightly lost.

"Do you know where you're going?" she asked, peering at the sleek towers of the financial district set against the pale evening sky. "Jon said the club is in Cambridge."

"Yes, but he told me this is the simplest route. Then we come back over the river at the Harvard Bridge."

"Ah. Storrow Drive. My favorite," she muttered through gritted teeth, while they raced along the narrow river-hugging roadway with the rest of the bumper-to-bumper seventy-mile-an-hour crazies.

Jon's world, she thought again, gripping the armrest with one hand, the upholstery with the other. On the radio, a jaunty Frank Sinatra was singing, "Come Fly With Me." She shut her eyes and didn't open them again until they'd crossed the Charles.

Jon's jazz club turned out to be a small street-level restaurant-cum-lounge in a nineteenth-century neighborhood that had undergone extensive gentrification. Brick side-walks and old-fashioned laurel-wrapped street lamps lent the area a Dickensian atmosphere.

Upon entering, Ivan put their coats on a rack by the door, then ushered Angela farther into the dimly lit room. Elegant pinecone wreaths graced the walls, their red plaid bows matching the heavy linen covering the tables. Each of those tables glowed with the light of a fat red candle in a glass shade ringed with holly.

Jon was seated at the bar facing the entrance. Angela noticed him immediately. As he did her. His back straightened, while his dark eyes traveled from her hair to her toes with slow deliberation. Had she overdressed? she wondered, feeling her color heighten.

As they approached, he swiveled around to face them, his long legs spraddled negligently, his drink held loosely in two hands.

He was wearing a white T-shirt with a dark tweed sports jacket, a combination that alone should have jangled Angela's sense of fashion decorum. Paired with well-worn jeans and black basketball sneakers, the likes of which she hadn't seen since the sixth grade, her sensibilities should have been outraged. Instead, Angela could only smile, struck by how good Jon looked. How relaxed, how confident and, yes, how elementally male.

"Are we late?" she asked, angry with herself for thinking along such lines.

"Not at all. We just got here ourselves."

Angela glanced up and down the bar.

"She's in the powder room," he explained.

"Not anymore," came a sultry voice. Angela looked to its source just as a willowy beauty wrapped her arms around Jon's waist and fitted herself against him.

"Angela, Ivan, this is my friend, Cynthia Gardner."

Smiling as warmly as she knew how, Angela shook the young woman's hand, which immediately returned to Jon's waist as if attached there by a spring. She introduced Ivan, who, to her undying relief, offered up a brief smile, and then Jon led them all toward their reserved table in front of the stage.

Just as she'd anticipated, Cynthia was gorgeous. Using her own five foot four as a measure, Angela figured her to be close to six feet tall. Her skin was like flawless porcelain, her makeup warm and muted, her scent exotically spicy. But her hair, a red-gold cloud of thick ringlets cascading to midback . . . her hair rendered her practically ethereal. Only belatedly did Angela even notice her outfit, a long-sleeved ballet leotard that emphasized her surprisingly full bust, and a swingy jungle-patterned skirt. As she walked, khaki tigers and giraffes prowled to and fro about her long shapely legs. Angela glanced down at her own outfit and felt like somebody's maiden aunt. But at least Ivan matched her, and that was all that really mattered.

They sat, ordered drinks, opened menus, talked about the drive down from Winston and the pleasant upturn in the weather, and throughout, Angela noticed, Cynthia never once removed her hand from Jon's thigh. Nor did he exhibit anything but devoted attention toward Cynthia. If anyone was scoring points on the couple meter, it was Jon and his walking Barbie of the jungle.

As unobtrusively as possible, Angela scooted her chair closer to Ivan's, but she absolutely refused to do anything with her hands but keep them folded in her lap.

"Well, this is nice." Cynthia's smile was dazzling. "I'm glad we finally got together. Jon has talked so much about you."

"Is that so?" Ivan sipped his vodka, his eyes shifting narrowly from face to face.

"Mmm. You and Jon lived across the street from each other. Right, Angela?"

"Uh, yes," Angela replied hesitantly.

"And is it true that when you were little, you actually did one of those gross blood-brother things?"

"I'm afraid so." Angela's glance grazed Jon's. She didn't want to get into memory-dredging tonight, and she sensed neither did he. That would defeat the purpose of this double date.

"Oh, I have to tell you what Ivan and I did yesterday," she said hurriedly.

Cynthia blinked a few times, surprised by the sudden switch in gears.

"We always go flea-marketing on Saturdays—Ivan collects all sorts of wonderful things—and yesterday we found a mint-condition stereopticon."

Jon's head tilted. "Really?"

Ivan leaned in and, with a smile that was genuine now, proceeded to describe in detail his collection of turn-of-the-century viewers.

Angela was pleased she'd found a way to bring him into the conversation. But before long, she noticed that Jon and Cynthia were straining to look interested. Not that Ivan's hobby was *uninteresting*, but he tended to dwell on the technical side of it, how things worked, their history. The wonderful old pictures themselves left him cold, Angela realized.

Fortunately the waiter appeared to take their order, and when he left, Jon leapt right into the void. "Did I tell you how Cynthia and I met?" He draped his arm across Cynthia's shoulder, while she gazed at him adoringly.

Angela was dismayed by the tightness in her chest. "Uh, no."

"Well, I was strolling through an outdoor market in Bahia one day..."

While Jon told his story, Angela nervously picked at the holly that encircled their table's candle. Had Jon finally found his perfect woman? Physically, Cynthia certainly filled the bill. Professionally it seemed she was at the top of her field, too. Angela couldn't even fault her personality. The woman was warm, charming and guilelessly open.

Evidently this evening really had been planned for them to get to know each other as couples. Which was fine with Angela. That was exactly what she'd set out to do herself, wasn't it? With a renewed sense of purpose, she buried her dismay and rejoined the conversation.

Cynthia had picked up a thread of Jon's story and was now spinning an elaborate complaint about the heat in Brazil and how hard it was to do a shoot there. Angela was a bit confused, not remembering how they'd arrived at that particular subject.

The waiter came with their food just then, and she thought she saw Jon's shoulders sag just a little in relief.

"Mmm. This food looks wonderful." Angela didn't have much of an appetite, but she tried to appear enthusiastic, anyway.

"It is," Jon added. "I try to eat here at least once a week."

"Do you eat out often?"

He nodded. "Especially the days I have double rehearsal."

Ivan looked from one to the other, a slight frown darkening his eyes. "Angela tells me you play with the Boston Symphony."

"Yes, I do."

"You know, Angela is applying for the position of conductor with the Winston Symphony..."

For some reason, her gaze was still locked with Jon's. At Ivan's words, they both froze—and then looked quickly away.

"It would be a tremendous favor if someone like you could write a letter of recommendation for her."

"Ivan!" She was mortified. "Jon's a very busy man."

"I'm sure he wouldn't mind, would you?"

Jon's lips parted, but he said nothing.

"Of course he wouldn't," Cynthia chimed in.

Angela moved her food around her plate. It was obvious that Jon did mind, and she knew precisely why. He didn't believe she was qualified.

"I'll see what I can do," Jon muttered. "So, have you seen any good movies lately?"

Hurt though she was, Angela still felt a weight lift. Finally a topic they could all safely sink their teeth into. As they talked about one favorite movie after another, she began to relax. She loved films, and soon her appetite returned. Luckily, she and Jon had seen almost all the same ones, a coincidence that fueled enough lively conversation to get them through to the end of the meal.

But finally Cynthia lay against Jon's shoulder and, in a jarring nonsequitor, inquired, "Why do you call her Angel?" The conversation came to a grinding halt.

"I've wondered about that myself," Ivan grumbled.

Angela met Jon's eloquent glance, and they both sighed in resignation. For several minutes now, Ivan and Cynthia had seemed to be growing bored with movies, anyway.

"I'm afraid I started calling her Angel as a taunt, then it just became habit. Her conscientiousness used to drive me crazy when we were kids. Homework always done. Clothing always tidy. She was punctual, kind, never swore or lied..."

"Ah, I see what you mean." Ivan smiled, obviously pleased with this explanation.

Cynthia draped an arm across Jon's chest and in a deep sardonic voice asked, "And what was my sweetie here like?"

Angela coughed behind her hand, smiling. "Your *sweetie* was an unadulterated devil."

"Was he?" Cynthia's green eyes widened expectantly. "Oh, do tell. I need some ammunition when he gets on my case. He says I whine, you know." With a roll of her expressive eyes, she clearly conveyed her opinion that the accusation was ridiculous.

Angela noticed Jon comb his fingers through his hair, several times, and for a moment wondered if the love of his life wasn't so ideal, after all.

"Ammunition, eh?" Maybe one story wouldn't hurt, and it just might give them a few more laughs. She really liked the easy mood they'd fallen into during dinner and hoped it would continue.

A moment later, Angela was deep into a story about an assembly that took place during her and Jon's junior year of high school.

"Our principal back then, Mr. Kelly, always gave a speech at assemblies. He was a sweet man, but unfortunately he could *not* tell a joke." Coffee arrived, and Angela was so animated by now, she was barely aware of spooning sugar and pouring cream.

"But during this one assembly, I realized the students were responding to him. I was sitting with the orchestra up front, below the stage, and I couldn't believe it. They were laughing at his dumb jokes. I mean, really keeling over. So, after about the fourth uproar, I turned around to find Jon, figuring he'd be just as lost as I was, and do you know what I saw?" She leaned toward Cynthia, the steam from her coffee warming her chin. "That monster was holding up a cardboard sign with the word 'Laugh' printed on it. He'd slipped it into his horn case, and everytime Mr. Kelly cracked a feeble joke, Jon, who, mind you, was sitting right under Mr. Kelly's nose, lifted his sign and the auditorium erupted."

Cynthia fell against Jon's arm, giggling helplessly.

Ivan, however, didn't seem to find the story one bit amusing. "Did the principal ever find out? Were you punished?"

"Afraid not." Jon smirked, sitting back comfortably. "To this day, Mr. Kelly probably dreams about that assembly with a big smile on his face."

Angela pointed with her dessert fork. "But some of the teachers saw."

"And?" Jon's smile broadened as his eyes locked with hers.

"And...nothing. That was the trouble with you, Jon. Everyone thought you were so charming you got away with murder."

Ivan was now tapping his spoon, rapidly, against his coffee cup. Was he angry about something? Angela blinked in confusion, and then, like a splash of cold water, it occurred to her: she and Jon had spent the better part of an hour talking either *to* each other or *about* each other.

That wasn't supposed to happen. She'd come here determined to prove he no longer fitted into her life. She'd planned to ignore him, avoid dredging up the past. Time had marched on, and she'd come here precisely to flaunt that fact. She'd wanted to knock away the nonsense he entertained about a renewed friendship and replace it with a crisp clear image of her and Ivan, instead.

She peeked up at Ivan. His expression had turned sullen again, his eyes shifting suspiciously from her to Jon. She reached over, squeezed his arm and smiled reassuringly, but his expression remained unchanged.

Angela was relieved when a young man carrying a saxophone interrupted.

"It's that time," he said, placing a hand on Jon's shoulder.

Jon pushed back his chair. "How long are you people staying?"

Angela glanced at Ivan. "One set."

"That's all?"

She nodded firmly.

Jon seemed disappointed but said nothing, simply rose and strode off to his waiting piano.

For the next forty minutes, Angela sat entranced. Each of the five musicians was excellent, but it was Jon who really held her attention. His improvisational solos took her into musical landscapes that were dazzling in their complexity and originality. Before long she was watching him exclusively, even when he wasn't in the spotlight.

In this setting, Jon was as loose and content as she'd ever seen him. And suddenly she also remembered how much he'd always needed jazz to unwind. Where ever had she gotten the idea it made him unfocused? If anything, he drew energy from playing this music.

She smiled, enjoying his joy vicariously. His thick black hair was mussed, his face relaxed. His whole body had shifted into another mode. Jon didn't just play; he caressed the piano keys, arousing a melody, awakening something in the rhythms that had been reluctant and elusive.

Angela slipped low in her chair, fingers pressed over her mouth, feeling an uncomfortable heat swirl through her.

They'd played music together all their lives, but never had she associated sensuality with what he did. This was something new, and she wasn't sure she liked it. She was paying attention to details that had no relevance to the music, such as the sheen of his hair under the lights, the starlike intensity lent to his eyes by the thickness of his lashes, the firm curve of his lower lip, the cleft in his chin. Had his fingers always been so long? Had he always worn clothing with such negligent aplomb? And the energy that drove him, had it ever come so near the surface?

She glanced at Cynthia and for the first time that evening honestly admitted her envy. What was it like, she wondered, being close to Jon now that he was a man? How did it feel to be touched so intimately by his magic?

The number came to a stunning end, and Angela applauded along with the rest of the attentive audience. She was feeling rather fuzzy and warm from the wine she'd had with dinner and was taken totally off guard when Jon lifted the microphone from his piano, swept the audience with his hot dark gaze and smoothly announced, "Tonight I have the pleasure of being here with my oldest and dearest friend..."

She sat up like a shot, her nerves ringing with tension.

"It's been a long time since we've seen each other, but I distinctly remember that when we were kids, she used to play a mighty mean flute."

Angela gripped the seat of her chair, her breathing arrested. *Don't do this to me, Jon,* she pleaded silently.

"I know she'll probably slug me later, but..." Jon reached under his piano and came up with a flute case she hadn't noticed before now. "Angel? How about it?" He looked directly at her, one dark eyebrow arched, and the audience, knowing a cue when they heard one, applauded. She felt dizzy, confused. Blood pounded in her ears. A decade had passed since she'd played in Jon's jazz band. They'd been high school kids then, and she really hadn't been any good. She shook her head and laughed, trying to put him off in a gracefully amiable fashion.

But she should have known better. Jon never gave up until he got what he wanted. "She's really very good, ladies and gentleman. She just doesn't know it yet."

The clapping became more insistent. She looked at Ivan and whispered, "Help me out of this." But Ivan was scowling and continued to scowl until she realized she'd get no help from that quarter. She got to her feet, and on legs that threatened to give out, walked into the warm circle of stage light.

"I'm not just going to slug you, Jon," she said, butting him with her shoulder, "I'm going to kill you." She hoped he realized how truly furious she was.

He handed over the flute with a debonair wink. She considered beating him with it right then and there, but she raised the cold metal to her chin, instead, and ran a quick scale up the keys. She wished she could disappear. She was painfully aware of the audience, aware of the racing of her heart and the dangerous shallowness of her breathing.

She wasn't used to playing jazz. It upset her, always had. Especially improvisation. Just as she'd never been much good at speaking in front of a class unless her speech was memorized, she feared music she hadn't studied and thoroughly rehearsed. While Jon could wing his way through almost anything, her need to be prepared was nearly phobic.

Jon muttered instructions to the other members of the group, returned to his piano, and they started to play a number she was familiar with. They played it simply, straightforwardly. Nevertheless, Angela let the music flow over her for a long while, too terrified to join in.

Jon's gaze lifted to hers repeatedly, but never questioning, never doubting. With her eyes locked on his, she finally raised the flute—and then lost courage again. Instead of dismay, he shot her one of his killer grins. Everything was okay, he seemed to be telling her; she had time, all the time in the world.

She smiled back, and on a momentary wave of confidence, raised the flute and this time began to play. It was difficult at first, and she made a point to play softly. She wished the music could flow from her as it did from Jon, naturally, spontaneously, but that just wasn't the way she'd been born.

Sweat trickled down her sides, and again she contemplated murder. Yet, despite her anger, she clung to Jon's gaze, afraid to let go. More than anything, watching him helped her wherever the music was headed.

Her hair lay damp on her neck and her knees still trembled badly, yet she sensed that her playing was growing more secure, her fingers more nimble. Hanging on Jon's warm supportive gaze, she began to feel connected to him, his strength flowing into her, her insecurity draining away. And although anxiety still fluttered in her stomach like the wings of a thousand butterflies, her mind grew ever more peaceful, letting go of logic, flowing deep, and deeper still, into a river of instinct. Jon smiled, small lines fanning out at the corners of his eyes—and the butterflies invaded her giddy heart.

The saxophone player launched into a solo then, carrying the melody like a slim ribbon into a thicket of complex improvisation. Within seconds it was barely recognizable. Angela clutched the flute under her chin as he played, her mood swinging to terror again at the possibility that she'd be expected to solo, too.

He finished all too quickly, and although she shook her head, the sax player still made it clear that it was her turn to play.

Stage lights blurred, and Angela grew light-headed. Not knowing what else to do, she turned to Jon for grounding. *Please, don't leave me out on a limb,* she begged him with her eyes. And he replied, *Everything's okay. You're safe.*

They played together, flute and piano intermingling in a dance she'd never learned the steps to. Sounds weaving, ducking, leaping around each other in an unpracticed and

utterly primal flow. And while she played, she was struck by
a disturbing realization. Sometime during the night, she had
entered Jon's world. Though she'd fought it, Jon had
somehow pulled her into his sphere, into his magic circle.
And even while she resented the seduction, she simultaneously experienced a moment of weightless floating joy in
what she was doing.

Their duo ended, the audience applauded, and Angela
was astonished to find herself laughing, the joy still jetting
through her.

The drummer took up the spotlight next. When he was
done, everyone returned to the straightforward melody, and
before she even realized it, the number was over. Jon came
around the piano and pulled her into a tight one-armed hug.
She leaned against his side, feeling warm and expansive and
so very, very clever.

"You were terrific." Jon's breath tickled her ear. "Now,
say good-night to the folks, Gracie."

Still laughing, Angela nodded into the sea of faces, then
floated back to her seat.

As the music resumed, Ivan leaned toward her and muttered something.

"What?" she asked distractedly.

"I said, I ought to take that jerk outside and give him
what he's looking for."

Suddenly the magic drained out of the night. "Ivan,
please."

"Please what? That was insensitive and totally uncalled-
for. Making a spectacle of you like that..."

"Oh. Was I that bad?"

"No, no, of course not." But from the way his eyes
avoided hers, she knew he didn't mean it.

Ivan was right, Angela thought, wrapping herself into a
tight ball of self-examination. She'd hated being up there,
hated being pushed to the limits of her abilities, and Jon
hadn't had any right doing that to her.

By the time the band took a break, she was only too eager to leave. Jon and Cynthia walked with them to the door.

"Thanks for making the trip down." Jon patted Ivan on the back.

In the wake of Ivan's silence, Angela answered, "Thanks for suggesting the idea."

Jon's mouth tightened as he looked from her to Ivan.

As usual, Cynthia had draped herself around Jon's torso, like a lizard around a warm stone. Angela was surprised she didn't just lift her feet off the floor and wrap her legs around him, too.

Almost immediately she chided herself for harboring such negative feelings toward the young woman. She was a lovely person. Really.

As if to prove the point, Cynthia smiled magnificently. "We'll have to do this again some time."

Angela didn't look at anyone. All she could think was, *Not on your life!*

She crossed the street with her arm tucked under Ivan's— one last attempt to appear the happy couple, one last picture to leave with Jon. Ivan unlocked his car, but just before getting in, Angela looked back toward the restaurant. Jon was still standing at the door, and even though Cynthia remained glued to his side, for a moment, one terribly vivid and totally inappropriate moment, Angela again felt connected to him.

"Get in, Angela." Ivan stood holding her door impatiently. "I want to get home. All that damn noise has given me a headache."

AT TEN MINUTES TO TWO, Angela's telephone rang. "Yes?" she gasped into the receiver.

"Angel. Hi."

"Jon?" She lay very still. "Where are you?"

"Home. Just got in." His voice was dark, deep, tired.

She switched on her bedside lamp. "What's up?"

"Nothing. Just called. Well, not much." He breathed heavily. "Aw, hell, how am I supposed to say this?"

She sat up, uneasy with the serious undertone in his voice. "Say what?"

"Angel, tonight when we were having dinner... remember when Ivan asked if I'd write a letter of recommendation for you?"

"Oh, that." Her voice—and heart—stopped.

"Maybe I should've said something then, but I didn't want to spoil the evening."

"What? Spit it out."

"Angel, don't get all upset now, but I can't write you a letter of recommendation."

"That's okay. I understand." Her voice rasped with heartache.

"No, I don't think you do. I can't recommend you because... because I've applied for the job myself."

CHAPTER FIVE

"WHAT DID YOU SAY?" Angela swung her bare feet to the floor, instantly awake.

"I sent in an application, too. Last August, when the ad first went out. Is that a problem? If it is, I'll call the search committee and tell them to remove my application."

Angela wanted to cry in sudden frustration. What could she say? Yes? That she wanted him to withdraw? That she didn't trust her chances against someone like Jon who got everything he ever tried for?

"Why on earth did you apply for the conductorship of the WSO? Don't you have enough on your plate yet?" Her voice was shakier than she wanted it to be.

He hesitated. "Actually, I applied before I heard from the BSO. It was only one of a few ventures. No rhyme or reason for it."

Angela sensed he was lying. "Are you still interested?"

"Well . . . it might be fun."

Fun? She sprang to her feet and stomped as far as the phone cord would reach. "And what makes you think you're qualified to conduct a symphony orchestra?" Fun. As if the WSO was some easy backwater lark!

"Like you, I've been in the trenches a long time, I know what makes a conductor effective, and I understand music."

"For your information, my qualifications happen to extend a little beyond just being in the trenches."

He must have heard the fury in her voice. The line hummed with silence for too long an interval.

"I said I'd remove my application."

Angela's relief came and went in a flash. "Don't insult me, Jon. Remove your application, and I'll never speak to you again."

"What's that supposed to mean?"

"Isn't it obvious? You apparently believe that if you stay in the race, I can't possibly win." She waited for a denial, but it never came.

"Why are you so upset? I don't even want the job."

"You just said you did. You said it would be *fun*." Her voice grated with sarcasm.

"Hey, listen, all I wanted to do was tell you I'd applied. I didn't want you hearing about it from somebody else and maybe thinking I'd pulled a fast one on you. The last thing I meant to do was start an argument. Honestly, Angel, you've got to be the most contrary person ever inflicted on the face of this earth."

"And you are undoubtedly the most arrogant. You're a musician, Jon, not a conductor."

"You're pacing. I can hear you pacing."

"So, arrest me!" With her free hand she bunched her hair into a fist and squeezed. She wanted to cry and hated herself for feeling that way. It was weak and irrational and everything she didn't want to be right now.

Jon sighed heavily. "It sounds like there's more to this than you're letting on, and I wish you'd tell me about it."

"It's nothing."

"Like hell. I picked up on this competition thing the other night at your place. Did somebody throw us into a ring when I wasn't looking? What's this all about, Angel?"

She groaned, sinking to the bed again. "You wouldn't understand if I gave you a blueprint."

"Oh. And what exactly is this mysterious thing I wouldn't understand?"

Angela dropped her head into her hand. "Me," she finally mumbled. "You don't know who I am, what's important to me or... or anything."

"Okay. I'll accept that as a possibility. I've been gone a while and people do change."

"But you've *never* known me. You've always ignored my needs, my strengths, my...my individuality. When we were kids, for instance, we always did what *you* wanted to do."

"That isn't true."

"It is. Think about it—the games we played, the people we hung around with. Granted, it wasn't entirely your fault. Everybody treated you special, and it went to your head. You got to believing that no one could possibly be as important as you."

"Wait. Could you slow down just a second? Talking to you is like running through a maze at sixty miles an hour. Are you trying to say you were miserable for eighteen years because I suppressed you?"

" 'Bulldozed' is a better description."

"Well, thank you very much."

"You're welcome, and yes, you did."

"Like when?"

"Like all the time. That dumb lip-sync contest, for example. Do you think I actually enjoyed that?"

"Yes. Yes, I do."

"Think again, Stoddard. I hated it. I was so nervous I almost threw up before going onstage. I also hated hang gliding, pizza with the works, winter camping, half the movies we saw and all the creeps you fixed me up with. And I most definitely hated playing with your band tonight."

Jon laughed incredulously. "You had the time of your life, and you know it. If you hadn't had me around to keep you loose all those years, you would've atrophied, like you're doing now with that stiff you call a boyfriend. Eevon."

Angela punched her pillow. "You big conceited jerk! Atrophied? *Atrophied?* That's just the sort of blind egocentric attitude I'm talking about. I lead a wonderful life, one I'm perfectly happy with, but because it's not what you would choose, you say I've atrophied. Well, you can go to hell."

"Nice language, Angel."

"Want to hear more?" She paused, shaking. It was the middle of the night, all of New Hampshire was asleep, and here she was, bellowing like a demented fishwife. "Look, all I meant to say was, *you* left Winston, not me. I've made a life here, and I don't appreciate your barging in after all this time, thinking it's okay to do whatever you want and I won't care."

"And I don't appreciate your assumption that I'm some egomaniacal Neanderthal."

"Well, if the shoe fits... You already have a job most musicians would kill for, but for you that's not enough. You've always been that way, Jon. You always needed to win one more award, prove you were the best in one more competition. And it didn't matter that you hurt people along the way. Your ambition was like this huge insatiable—"

"Hey!" His shout made her jump. "I don't have to take any more of this swill. Call me when your brain comes back from the cleaners."

"Don't hold your breath." She slammed down the phone, but not fast enough to beat him to it.

BEFORE ANGELA HAD TIME to sort out all the perplexing emotions that had surfaced during her argument with Jon, it was Wednesday. She taught at the high school on Wednesdays—music theory fourth and fifth periods, string orchestra eighth.

As the last of her students filed out of the practice room, she decided that anyone involved with three different musical groups during the month of December had to be totally crazy. This Friday night was the high school concert, next Tuesday the college performed, on the following Sunday the WSO did its thing, and for each of those events Angela still had a thousand details to arrange. It was not a good week, she decided, leaning over the water fountain to swallow an aspirin.

Not that she didn't enjoy her work; she did. She just wished there wasn't so much of it. There was a side to her that longed to be more domestic, longed to have time to prepare for the holidays with the care her sister took, decorating sugar cookies and walking into the woods for greens, instead of slapping a homogenized, store-bought wreath on her door. And though she didn't often admit it, she also wished she had people in her life to do those things for—a husband, children.

She stepped away from the fountain and wiped her mouth with the back of her hand. Actually, her yearnings for family weren't as beyond reach as she made them out to be. Ivan had talked about marriage on several occasions, making it amply clear that their living together would only be a preliminary. She also knew he didn't expect her to work after they were married, at least not in the fragmented hectic manner she was accustomed to now. He wanted a gracious home, well-tended children, relaxed mealtimes—things she wanted herself. All she had to do was give him a yes.

What she decided to do at that moment, however, was take another aspirin. She couldn't think about a decision of that magnitide just yet. She had too many errands to run, and then she had to get braced for tonight's WSO rehearsal—and facing Jon again, if he still planned to attend. She was pretty sure he would. It all made sense to her now—his volunteering to be guest soloist, his sitting in on the rest of the concert and coming to rehearsal when he didn't have to. He was trying to make his presence felt, not only among the musicians whom he believed he'd soon be leading, but also with Mr. Beech, who held perhaps the most influential vote on the search committee.

Angela swallowed the second aspirin, then filled a long-spouted container and watered the six lushly blooming poinsettia plants on the window ledge. She told herself she shouldn't worry. She had the qualifications; Jon didn't. And she and Mr. Beech were pals. As crusty as the old guy was, he liked her, admired her, and she knew he'd go to bat for her no matter who her competition was.

But she worried nonetheless. Jon was flashy. Jon was a name. Handsome. Famous by local standards. He also possessed a charm the board would not be impervious to.

The board was made up of four middle-aged women whom Angela tried to see as indispensable philanthropists, giving generously of their time to keep the orchestra financially solvent. Yet she couldn't deny that their self-important posturing and lack of any real musical appreciation could sometimes try her patience, and she was sure they were going to roll over and die when they met Jon.

Unless he withdrew his application.

She picked up an empty gum wrapper from the floor and dropped it into the basket. She'd told him not to withdraw his application, but he'd said he would. A couple of times. Would he? Probably not. He didn't understand how important the job was to her, didn't understand it wasn't his natural right to take whatever he wanted. Besides, he never withdrew from a challenge.

As angry as she was with him, though, she still felt bad about the argument they'd had the other night. She wished she hadn't reacted so emotionally. It was totally unlike her to fly off the handle like that. But the WSO meant so much to her she hadn't been able to control herself. Words had simply poured out helter-skelter. Hurtful words.

She didn't resent Jon's success. She never had. So why had she stomped all over it, raving about his insatiable ambition? And what *was* this competition thing all about?

Angela had no answers. Nor did she know how she was going to get through tonight's rehearsal. She'd skip if that was possible, but unfortunately she was chairman of the Christmas party and still had money to collect from several people.

She sighed, unplugged the artificial Christmas tree, picked up her briefcase and turned to leave. A second later her heart was in her mouth.

Jon was standing in the doorway, arms crossed over his chest, the upturned collar of his leather jacket framing his handsome face. Under the jacket, he was wearing a thick gold-toned sweater over brown corduroy jeans. Everything about him was warm and earthy, she thought before remembering to scowl.

"What are *you* doing here?"

His dark starlike eyes traveled the length of her, making her conscious of the trim plum-colored suit she was wearing. His gaze lingered on her matching high-heeled shoes before returning slowly to her face. She wondered what he saw. All grown up and polished? Or atrophied?

He pushed away from the doorway and strolled toward her. "Rehearsal," he explained.

She glanced at her watched. "Bravo. You're five hours early."

"That right?" He looked good, rested, as if their argument hadn't cost him any sleep. Angela's anger heated to a healthy simmer.

"How'd you find me?"

"Easy. I went to the office and said I had a conference with you concerning my kid brother." Jon actually had the audacity to grin. "The secretary was most obliging. Found your schedule, gave me directions, even offered to walk me."

"I bet she did."

Jon stepped onto her podium and scanned the untidy arc of metal chairs and music stands before him.

"Didn't it occur to you," she said, "that I might not want to see you?"

"No," he returned readily. "You know, I could get used to this. What a sense of power."

The simmer rose to a boil. "Oh, really. Do you want this job, too?" She yanked on her coat and tried to hurry past him, but he reached out and caught her by the arm.

"Angel, wait. You know damn well the reason I'm here. Don't make it difficult."

Angela looked him up and down with as much scorn as she could muster. "I don't know what you're talking about."

"Knock it off. In all the years we've known each other, we've never fought the way we did the other night, never, and frankly I don't like it."

"Well, that's too bad. I can't take back what I said just because you don't like it."

"True, but maybe you'll accept an apology."

"I see no point."

"Angel, the point is, I don't want us to be angry with each other."

She slung her purse strap over her shoulder. "Fine. We're not angry."

He fell into step beside her. "Good. Then let's go for coffee."

Closing her eyes, she blew out a sigh. "I don't want any coffee."

He pushed open the heavy glass door, and the December afternoon hit her with a cold damp blast. She huddled into her coat, thinking a cup of coffee would be glorious right about now, and scanned the parking lot for her car. Jon's Mercedes was parked right next to it.

"Angel, stop a minute." He swung her around to face him. She watched the breeze lift his hair off his forehead and was again struck by how compellingly handsome he was.

"What!" she asked with sharp impatience.

"What's wrong with you? Can't you accept a simple apology? I'm sorry you led such a rotten repressed existence being my friend. I'm sorry I made you play music you didn't like, sorry I had the arrogance to apply for the same job you did, even though I didn't know you'd applied. I'm even sorry I like olives on my pizza."

Angela threw up her hands. "There. See? You can't even apologize right."

She turned and marched off toward her car, but not three steps later she stopped again, uncertain if she was seeing right. "What the...?" She inched closer. "Oh, my Lord!"

The entire back seat of her automobile was filled with red and green balloons, their big bright faces pressed gaily to the windows.

"Angel, what happened to your car?" Jon asked, a study in innocence.

She slowly walked a circle around the vehicle, trying to cling to her anger. She didn't want balloons. They were childish and didn't change a thing between them.

"You really ought to lock your car." Jon folded his arms and leaned against her fender. "Anybody could get in."

For one fleeting moment she considered the possibility that Ivan might have perpetrated this whimsical stunt, but the thought dissipated almost instantly. Ivan was too practical, a virtue she normally admired.

Jon opened the door, watching her with a twinkle of mischief in his eyes.

"Did you do this?" She tried to infuse her words with disgust. "What a waste of good money. These things are expensive." She thought of pulling the balloons out, letting them go and destroying his gesture. She didn't want to be cajoled.

But she couldn't. No one had ever given her a gift of balloons before, and they were delightful.

Jon reached around her, plucked a red balloon by its string and drew it out of the car. "Come on, lighten up, Angel," he admonished, bopping her over the head.

"Stop it!"

"Okay, that was childish." He composed his demeanor, the balloon now looking out of place in his long manly hand. "Obviously your anger runs deeper than I thought, and I'm diminishing its importance by thinking a few balloons are going to mollify you."

"Well, thank you, Einstein." She tossed her briefcase and purse onto the front seat, tucked up her coat and attempted to get in. Jon, however, was standing in her way.

"Since I'm here five hours early," he said, his fingers working at the lumpy knot on the neck of the balloon, "and since I have nowhere to go, how about letting me hang around with you?"

His closeness was beginning to disorient her. "Jon, I have a dozen errands to run between now and rehearsal. I can't stop everything just to socialize."

"Of course not. I don't expect you to." As serious as a judge, he lifted the untied balloon to his lips, released a spurt of helium and swallowed. "What I was hoping—" abruptly, his deep voice changed, leaping to a high squeaky register like a record shifting into a faster speed "—was that I could just stay at your place."

Angela's breathing came hard and heavy. She so wanted her reaction toward his juvenile behavior to be anger, but a moment later she was fighting not to smile, and a moment after that, fighting not to laugh.

"So how about it?" he squeaked. "I'll even spring for the beer and pizza."

Angela felt the last of her anger desert her. "What am I going to do with you, Stoddard?" she groaned.

For a few seconds, he fixed her with an enigmatic look, and then he grinned.

AT A RED LIGHT two blocks from the school, Jon beeped his horn and motioned for Angela to let him pull in front of her. When the light changed, she waited, perplexed, as he took the lead. At the next corner, instead of going straight, he turned left. This wasn't the way to her place. It wasn't even a shortcut.

What it was, she soon realized, was the route to their old neighborhood. She tapped her hand on the steering wheel, her resistance rising in a hot aching tide.

"What are you doing, Jonathan?" she complained while her car idled in the middle of Elm Street. He'd already pulled to the curb.

"Just decided to come take a look. I haven't seen the place since my parents moved." He unfolded himself from his sports car and gazed up at the large Victorian that had been his childhood home.

Reluctantly, Angela parked in front of him but kept her engine running. "This is stupid, Jon," she said, leaning out her window. "It's maudlin. Like visiting a cemetery."

He seemed not to hear her but went on walking the property frontage, peering into the backyard, then up to the turreted roof, then back down to the deep wraparound porch. Someone had covered the front door in gold foil and wide red ribbon to resemble a Christmas gift. "Hasn't changed much, has it?"

Her gaze moved across the street to the green-shuttered, white-clapboard colonial where she had been raised. She swallowed.

"This was a nice place to grow up, wasn't it?"

"Jon, let's go."

"I will. In a minute. Lord, will you look at the size of that tree." He turned slowly. Then, "Holy crow! Angel, look."

"What now?"

"The Thurgood house is for sale."

Angela peered through her fogging windshield as he jogged a long diagonal across the street. Groaning in resignation, she turned off her engine and followed.

The house that their sometime friends, Robby and Lisa Thurgood, had lived in would have been impressive in any setting. On this comfortably casual middle-class street, it approached castlehood. Angela was surprised to discover that time had not diminished her reaction to the sprawling English Tudor one bit.

Jon was standing in front of one of the street-facing, diamond-paned windows. The library windows, Angela recalled. He cupped his hand around his eyes and looked in.

"They're gone. The place is empty," he said.

She was more than slightly curious herself now. She crossed the frozen lawn, slipped between the shrubbery and peered through the parlor window. A huge stone fireplace, one of four in the house, faced her from the opposite wall. "Hmm. I wonder where they went."

"Frankly, I don't care. They were such tightwads. Remember the half-rotted apples they used to give out at Halloween?" Jon chuckled, a deep-throated sound that brought a grudging smile to Angela's lips.

"But they made up for it at Christmas. Three trees, remember? One in the parlor, another in the breakfast room, and then the fifteen-footer in the foyer. This was definitely a good Christmas house."

"I'll give them that." Jon walked back down the brick path, turning several times to give the place another speculative look. "Thanks for humoring me, Westgate. We can go run your errands now."

"Gee. Thanks a bunch."

They ate at the small round table in her balloon-festooned kitchen, watching a light snow sift down through the bright outdoor lights on her patio.

Angela remained rather quiet throughout, letting Jon take the reins of the conversation, because quite honestly she didn't understand what was happening between them. She'd been so angry with him just hours before, and if she thought about it objectively, she still had every reason to be angry. Nothing had changed. Unfortunately, what objective reason didn't understand was that it was nearly impossible to stay mad at someone who refused to be mad in return.

"By the way—" Jon closed the empty pizza box "—another reason I came up early... Can I interest you in spending the weekend in Boston?"

"Again? We were just there."

Jon rubbed his dark jaw, his day's growth of beard rasping under his hand. "No, not like last time. How about coming down on Friday night and staying over. That'll give us time to do the city on Saturday. Then at night, well, there's the symphony. You can return on Sunday."

"Oh, Jon, it sounds wonderful." Angela propped her chin on her hand. "But I don't foresee Ivan enjoying such an extended stay in the city."

Jon's face hardened. "Does that mean you wouldn't consider coming by yourself?"

"Jon!"

"No, I guess you wouldn't."

"Well, how do you think that'd go over? Not just with Ivan. What about Cynthia?"

He made a low growling sound of frustration. "You're right, you're right. Ask Ivan to come, anyway. You never know."

But she did know. Ivan disliked going away for weekends. Spending the weekend at Jon's—well, that was almost laughable.

Jon glanced at his watch. "Okay, kid. It's that time."

"Already?" Angela rose with a doleful sigh. They cleared the table quickly and headed for the door. But just before leaving the kitchen, she plucked a balloon down from the ceiling, found the scissors and snipped off the end.

"Okay, now I'm ready." Her sudden chipmunk voice stopped Jon in his tracks. "Will you get my coat out of..." She couldn't go on, succumbing to a fit of laughter.

Jon smiled at her, a deeply pleased smile, she thought. "Westgate, you're incorrigible."

"Thanks. And I owe it all to you." She let the balloon go and giggled again as it swooped about the room, taking a final nosedive into a lamp shade.

Rehearsal ran long, and even when it was over, Angela still had Christmas-party business to finish. She was yawning by the time Jon pulled up in front of her condo.

"Would you like to come in for something to drink? Coffee? Hot cocoa?" She didn't expect him to say yes. He looked pretty tired himself.

"Sure. Cocoa sounds good."

"Oh. Oh, well, sure, okay."

"Is that a problem? I can keep right on going . . ."

"No. Don't be silly." But she knew a problem did exist. She wanted him to come in. She didn't want their time together to end just yet, and that frightened her. She couldn't remember changing her mind about the status of their friendship. As far as she was concerned, it was still a dead issue. What was Jon doing to her resolve? For while her mind could tick off lots of reasons she was better off without him, her heart felt distinctly otherwise.

"Does this fireplace work, or is it just for show?" Jon called from the living room.

"It works. Why?" She poured milk into a pan and set it on the burner.

"It's chilly in here."

"So turn up the heat."

"Okay."

But when Angela walked into the living room, a log was blazing away. "Gee, make yourself at home, why don't you." She shook her head disparagingly, set down the tray and turned on the stereo. The soft-rock station she sometimes listened to came on, but the station's call letters, which she'd programmed into the machine, were not what she expected. She leaned in to get a better look, then let out an irrepressible laugh. Instead of "WXEB," it now read, "YECH." Would Jon leave no corner of her life untouched?

She composed her expression and turned to find him watching her. Her heart did an unexpected stutter. "It took me three weeks to learn how to program that machine," she complained. "How did you do it so fast?"

He only smiled.

She sat beside him on the sofa, tucking up her legs, and for a long while, they stared at the leaping flames in companionable silence.

"Jon, I'm sorry I blew up the other night." She looked aside, puzzled by her admission. "That's not to say I'm taking back what I said," she added quickly. "I meant it. Well . . . some of it."

Jon rested his hand on the back of her neck. It felt warm and comforting. "Shh. Let's drop it."

Angela nodded, trying not to pay attention to the shivers his gently stroking fingers were creating. "Before we do, though, I have one question."

"What's that?" He lay his head against the sofa back, his dark eyes half-closed.

"What do you intend to do with your application?"

He cast her a sleepy smile. "If you think I'm going to answer that, you're crazy."

"But why?"

"Because you'd damn me whether I withdrew or didn't withdraw. Either way you'd find some excuse to be angry."

"You mean I have to spend the next three weeks in suspense?"

"Uh-huh." He set his empty mug on the end table. "Hey, babe?"

"What?" She was tapping her foot in a sharp nervous rhythm.

"I think you should've made coffee, instead of hot milk."

Her tapping stopped. She turned and studied him in deepening alarm.

"What time do you get up, Angel?"

"Why?"

"Because I have to be at work by nine."

Angela swallowed convulsively. "But you can't stay here."

Jon pried off his boots and lay on his side, his legs slung heavily over her lap and a throw pillow tucked under his cheek. "Wake me by seven, will you, please?"

Angela lifted his legs and stood, folded her arms and huffed. His stubbled cheeks were flushed from sitting by the fire, and the thought crossed her mind that he'd probably catch cold if she turned him out now, to say nothing of the accident he might get into, given his state of alertness.

"Well, you might as well use the spare room." She sighed. "You'll wake up with a stiff back if you sleep here."

ANGELA WAS IN the upstairs bathroom brushing her teeth the next morning when the phone rang.

"Angel?" Jon called up the stairs.

Her heart lurched at the sound. It was so odd having him here, part of her everyday routine.

"Are you able to get that?" he asked.

"No. Will you? I'll be right down." She rinsed her brush, popped it into its holder and hurried down the stairs, carrying her shoes.

Standing at the bottom, Jon was frowning eloquently. Her steps slowed and before she could check herself, she muttered, "Oh, no." Jon's frown deepened.

She took the receiver from his hand and pulled in a shaky breath. "H-hello?"

"Angela, love. You forgot to call me last night."

"Good morning, Ivan. How are you?"

"Not too happy. Why didn't you call? I was worried." Ivan was speaking words of concern, but Angela only heard their steely undertone. Her mouth went dry.

She glanced toward the kitchen where Jon had thoughtfully retreated. What was Ivan thinking? Obviously she had to face the issue head-on.

"Jon stayed over last night. Rehearsal ran late, and he was so tired I was afraid he'd fall asleep at the wheel. I...I insisted he get some rest before heading back to Boston." She made a conscious effort to smile and speak in a confident manner.

"I know," Ivan returned. "I drove by your place around midnight and saw his car."

The floor seemed to dissolve from under Angela's feet. Ivan had taken to checking up on her now? "W-why didn't *you* call me?"

Ivan chuckled. "That's the question you have to answer, not I. You're the one with the, ahem, overnight guest."

Angela felt her cheeks warming. "I hope you're not thinking what I think you're thinking."

Again he laughed, a sound like dry leaves in a winter wind. "Yes, well, all I know is, within one short week that so-called friend of yours is sleeping over, something I haven't been able to do in six long months. So you'll have to excuse me if my nose is slightly out of joint."

She felt knotted with frustration. "There's no base of comparison between you two. Jon and I . . . we're just good friends." She pulled up short. What had she said? Did she mean those words? And if she didn't, why had they poured out so easily?

"Yeah, right. And I suppose you're about to tell me all the motels in the area were filled."

Angela pressed a hand to her forehead. "Listen, can we continue this later? I don't know what else to tell you."

"Fine, fine. I'm sorry I interrupted whatever you two were doing." His voice slithered with innuendo.

She was too hurt and angry to muster a defense. "See you on campus," she said quickly and hung up the phone.

Jon was at the kitchen sink rinsing their breakfast dishes.

"You don't have to do that. Leave them, Jon. Please. You've got a long drive ahead of you, commuter traffic . . ."

He turned from the sink and pinned her with his dark incisive stare. "What are you doing going out with that fool?"

Angela's back straightened. "That's inappropriate and totally uncalled for."

"Is it?"

"Yes." As angry as she was with Ivan, her pride still demanded that Jon see them as a happy couple. "I don't know how that phone conversation came across, but honestly, Ivan was just curious why you'd stayed over, that's all. Everything's fine." She moved to place her coffee mug in the sink but dropped it, instead. She stared at the broken pieces and felt an unexpected stinging in her eyes.

Jon let out a long tight breath. "Great. Everything's fine. Except that you're wound tighter than a top whenever he's around, and I can't help thinking you don't belong with him. I've known guys like Ivan, guys who are so possessive that eventually their girlfriends can't even sneeze without them demanding a written report. Is that what you want, Angel?"

Angela spun on him, resentment rising with unexpected force. "At least he cares." The silence between them throbbed with the unspoken accusation.

"It only looks like caring, babe."

"Jon, mind your own business, okay?"

"That's precisely what I'm doing," he said, his stare drilling into her until she couldn't hold it any longer. Then he turned and walked out to the living room where he shrugged on his jacket. "Thanks for letting me crash."

She tossed her hair back, not answering. Jon opened the front door and paused.

"Call if you need me."

"I won't."

He nodded, thoughtful. "I hope not."

As soon as he was gone, Angela pitched a chair pillow at the door and wailed a long frustrated "Aargh!" She didn't need Jon Stoddard, didn't need him telling her what was wrong with her love life, either. It was fine. Jon just didn't understand commitment—except to himself and his career. He didn't understand someone who cared as much as Ivan did, someone who was content with small-town life and unafraid of words like "roots" and "forever." It wasn't in his nature.

But as her anger ebbed, a pensive tension took its place. If nothing was wrong with her and Ivan's relationship, then why didn't she want him to move in with her? Why did she have this unshakable feeling that their romance had gone just about as far as she cared for it to go?

CHAPTER SIX

THE CHRISTMAS CONCERT at Winston High was in full swing. Angela's string orchestra had gone on first and was now scattering backstage while a noisy crew rearranged risers for the chorus. Directing them from the sidelines, Angela bit her lip trying not to laugh as the artificial snow, meant to fall during the singing of "Winter Wonderland," began to sift down on them.

"Angela?"

"Yes?" she replied, swinging around.

"Good job. Excellent." The young, newly hired director of the marching band was holding out his hand to congratulate her. With a laugh he decided to hug her, instead.

"Thanks, Bob."

"Now, if only I can get my bunch to do even half as well . . ."

"They will. Have faith."

He crossed his fingers, both hands. "Well, I'd better go check on them in the band room. See you later."

"Sure enough." She smiled happily, watching him hurry off. Angela was in exceptionally good spirits tonight. Being surrounded by dozens of exuberant teenagers was part of the reason, but improved relations with Ivan also helped.

After the words she'd had with him on the phone yesterday morning, she'd dreaded meeting up with him later. But when she'd walked into her office, a vase of carnations had been sitting on her desk, along with a note of apology. Ivan had apologized in person, too, and after her last class, had taken her to dinner. He couldn't have been more attentive.

After he'd dropped her off, Angela had sat for a long time examining their relationship. This was the Ivan she'd known for most of the time they'd been dating.

She'd started seeing him right after her mother died, a time when she'd been feeling rather lost and alone. But Ivan had been there for her, dependably phoning every night, stopping by to have supper, not only filling a void but making her forget it with the ardor of his pursuit. She didn't know what she would've done without him.

Remembering this, she realized the changes in his behavior had come about only recently, and perhaps *she* was the one who'd brought them on. Without realizing it, maybe she'd become inattentive, causing him to feel justifiably slighted. As for the argument they'd had because of Jon's sleeping over, upon reflection she decided that most men would've been just as upset as Ivan. She'd finally gone to bed firmly resolved to put more effort into their relationship.

Now she watched the chorus members, aglow in their festive red robes, file out onto the stage. When the last had taken her position on the risers, Angela gave their leader an encouraging thumbs-up and turned, bumping right into a solid chest.

"Oh. Ivan." She laughed. "What are you doing here?"

He didn't return her good humor. "I thought I'd come by and take you out for a drink. You are done here, aren't you?"

Angela opened her mouth, then closed it again. Her eyes wandered over the lively backstage crowd—musicians, baton twirlers dressed as elves, a portly senior in a Santa suit. She didn't have any specific duties left, but she'd wanted to stay. Being with these lively teenagers was doing wonders for her sagging spirits. It took her back vividly to her own high school days, spent right here in these corridors and classrooms, on this very stage. She was even beginning to catch some Christmas spirit, something she'd given up on this year.

Then again, she *had* made that resolution.

"I'll get my coat," she said with a sinking heart.

On the way out the back door, Ivan asked, "Who was that guy?"

Angela was trying to hear the chorus's first selection, a moving a cappella rendition of "The Christmas Song." "What guy?" she asked distractedly.

"The one who was so chummy."

"Bob?" She peered into Ivan's stern gray eyes and felt herself tense. "You can't be serious. That was just an innocent hug between colleagues. He was congratulating me on the kids' performance."

Ivan snorted contemptuously.

"For heaven's sake, he's married, Ivan. Blissfully so."

"Maybe you think it was innocent, but I'm a man and I know how so-called innocent hugs affect other men. It's flirting, Angela, out-and-out flirting, and I'll have none of it, do you hear?"

Angela stopped in her tracks, the apprehension she'd been feeling deepening to a chill. She'd thought she'd reasoned out Ivan's behavior last night, but this wasn't natural. She contemplated arguing against his irrational accusations, but because they *were* irrational, she doubted even the best defense would do any good.

Of course, she could apologize, reassure him it would never happen again. But giving in suddenly seemed terribly unappealing. She'd only be reinforcing an attitude that was totally invalid.

"Ivan, I hope you don't mind, but I'm not going for a drink, after all."

His brow lowered. "Going back in there, aren't you?"

That was precisely what she wanted to do, but she wouldn't. "No, I'm tired and I'm going home."

"Fine. I'll—"

"No. I'm going alone. I also think—" she swallowed "—I think we should give each other a rest this weekend."

"What?" His eyes chilled to steel.

"We need some space. Maybe the holidays are getting to us, I don't know, but we need to take a break from each other."

"Permanently?"

"That's not what I'm saying. Just…this weekend. It's for our own good. I'm sure we'll appreciate each other a whole lot more after a rest."

"But what'll you do?"

She shrugged. "Christmas shopping. Decorating. And of course, with the semester closing this week, I have a brief-case full of blue books to grade. Don't worry. I'll keep busy and so will you." She opened her car door.

"This is absurd!"

But she was done arguing. She got in quickly, shut her door and sped off.

Angela lit lights in all her downstairs rooms when she got home, poured herself a cinnamon schnapps and turned on the radio. She was still shaking. She hoped she'd done the right thing. It was so hard to tell anymore.

She took a fortifying sip from the glass in her hand, her gaze sweeping the room. What *would* she do this weekend? For while there was certainly plenty to do, she didn't feel like doing any of it.

She paced to the front window to stare at the lights shining from other town houses—white, green, red—their cheery glow only intensifying her growing sense of isolation.

Her mother had moved here because she'd been worried about Angela. She'd wanted to leave her in a place she could handle. Angela shook her head regretfully. It seemed her entire life had been overshadowed by an awareness of her parents' age and infirmity. With a waiting for their death.

She wished they'd stayed at the old house. Although her mother's intentions had been good, this cookie-cutter development had never felt like home. Tonight it felt like a burden, a weight crushing the air from her lungs.

When had everything closed in so tightly? And why was she suffering this sudden need to break free?

Angela closed the curtains with a hard yank, deciding she'd be far better off immersing herself in some task. She lifted her briefcase onto the coffee table and snapped open the locks, but a moment later she was sinking into the spot on the sofa that Jon seemed to favor.

Overhead, a few bright balloons still bobbed against the ceiling, swaying gently in the heat rising from the registers. How she wished he was here.

Angela covered her eyes and let the tears gather. "Oh, Jon," she whispered, her throat tight and achy. She shouldn't want to be his friend anymore. It was an impossible situation for so many, many reasons. Yet, at this moment there was no one on earth she wanted to talk to more than Jon.

Impulsively, she hauled herself off the couch and went to the phone. She was well aware that he might hang up on her, and her hands shook as she dialed. She'd practically thrown him out the last time he was here, telling him to keep his opinions of her and Ivan to himself, and when he'd offered his help, she'd tossed it right back.

"Jon? Hi!" She sounded like a cheerleader. A nasally sounding cheerleader.

"Hey, kid." A smile warmed his voice.

"Hi!" she repeated. "I didn't know if you'd be in."

"Been in for hours. We do a matinee on Fridays."

"Ah. Good concert?"

"Out of this world. Strauss's Alpine Symphony."

"Great, because you know what? I have the chance to attend tomorrow night's performance, after all." She waited for a response, but the line went silent. "That is, if the invitation is still open." *He knows something's wrong,* she thought. *Damn, he knows.*

"Of course. How many tickets will you need?"

"Uh, just one. Ivan . . . has something at the college. A b-banquet. But he insists I go and enjoy the weekend."

"He does?"

"Sure. You know how it is. There are just some times when people have too many commitments and have to go their own ways." She was almost choking on her words.

To her undying relief, Jon only replied, "Can I expect you tonight?"

"It's kind of late. How about tomorrow morning?"

"Sure. But you will be staying over on Saturday night, won't you?"

She hesitated, pulses thrumming. "I guess."

"Terrific. Got a pen? I'll give you directions."

When he finished, she stared at her handwriting and wondered if she'd ever be able to decipher the nervous scratches. Maybe it was a sign she shouldn't be doing this.

"Is Cynthia going to the concert, too?"

"Uh-uh. She's on a job out of town."

Angela wet her parched lips. "That's too bad. It would be nice to have someone to sit with."

"Angel, is everything okay with you?"

"Sure. Great," she answered, falsely bright. "Well, I'd better get some sleep. See you tomorrow." She hung up the phone and butted her head against the wall until it hurt.

THE APARTMENT Jon subletted was on the first floor of an elegant three-and-a-half-story brick house near Harvard Square. Angela rang the bell, and before she could even step back, the door opened with a vigorous *whoosh*.

"Hey! You made it." Jon was wearing gray cords and a heavy black sweater that looked hand-knit. He was clean-shaven; his thick curling hair, still damp from a recent shower, looked remarkably neat, and he smelled wonderful, a combination of soap and something cinnamon.

"Come in," he finally said, making her realize she was gaping.

The apartment was large and surprisingly bright, with a feeling of airiness created by the high ceilings, white walls and broad expanses of polished oak floor.

"Jon, this place is wonderful."

"Mmm. I'm enjoying it. Unfortunately, the couple who lives here'll be back after Christmas."

"What are you going to do then?"

"Not sure yet. Hey, let's take your stuff into the guest room and I'll show you around."

He led her toward one of two bedrooms, where she lay her garment bag over a bed.

"I hope I'm not interrupting anything. If you have to practice for tonight..."

"No, I'm done. Already put in my three hours."

Angela glanced at her watch, amazed by his industry.

He offered her coffee, which she declined, and took her on a hasty tour. On a windowsill over the kitchen sink, she spotted a row of photographs.

"Oh, your parents." She smiled, picking up one of the small framed pictures. "How are they?"

"Same as ever. Extremely busy. Still running their music shop. Oh, and now my mother's into scuba diving."

"They look wonderful." Angela peered intently at the photograph, at the handsome dark-eyed man Jon resembled, at the vibrantly smiling woman from whom he'd inherited his free spiritedness. "I miss them," she said without intending to.

"You'll just have to visit them sometime, then, won't you?"

"Mmm." She put the photo back and scanned the others. "Oh, gosh." Recognizing her senior-class picture, she grimaced, even though she was terribly pleased at having been included. "Who are these other people?"

"Friends I made in my travels, people I played with on the road. That was Vienna. That one there, Japan."

"You haven't talked much about those years. Do you miss it, being on the road, seeing all those exciting places?"

He was quiet a long while, eyes fixed but unfocused. "It was a wonderful experience. I learned a lot. But it catches up with you after a while. Living out of a suitcase, the tiredness..." He shook his head. "You may not believe this, but after a while I really got to missing New England. Missing Winston."

"You're right. I don't believe it." Angela was puzzled when he didn't return her humor, when his face continued to sober.

"One day I woke up and realized I didn't own a damn thing, Angel. Only my clothes, those pictures, a hot plate. Even worse, I didn't belong anywhere."

Angela would've liked to believe he was serious, and maybe right now he was, but she knew the mood wouldn't last. Jon didn't know the meaning of staying put. The only thing that was uncertain was how long it would be before he left. Two years? Six months? A frown tightened her brow. Already she knew his leaving was going to hurt.

"Ah, well," she sighed, "if you want to keep moving, you've got to travel light. Right?"

He blinked, emerging from his thoughts. "Oh...right." But he smiled only halfheartedly.

She followed him back to the living room, where he unhooked his leather jacket from a coat tree.

"Are you still up for doing the city?" he asked. The soft December light angling over his face unexpectedly caught her attention. Jon had always been handsome, but now his looks were overpowering. For a moment, she almost forgot to answer him.

"I—I'm looking forward to it."

"Good. I am, too."

Angela zipped up her pink ski jacket, a garment she didn't wear often, and pulled a pair of matching angora mittens from her pocket. From her other pocket, Jon pulled fuzzy pink earmuffs and, obviously quite amused by the things, slipped them on her head. "Cute, Westgate. Very cute." When he tucked and smoothed her hair, her breath grew alarmingly shallow.

"So, where would you like to go?" he asked.

She was sure her cheeks were as pink as her outfit by now, but she refused to make anything of it. Her reaction to Jon was perfectly understandable. He'd grown physically into a very compelling man, and she was simply having trouble reconciling the new with the old.

She reminded herself again of the reason she'd come here. A couple of days away from Winston would do her and Ivan a world of good. This weekend would relax her, recharge her batteries, and when she returned, their relationship would be better than before.

"Choose something." He opened the door. "The Museum of Fine Arts? Faneuil Hall? The aquarium?"

"So much to do, so little time." She felt his hand at the small of her back and shivered. "Faneuil Hall?"

"Okay."

"Are you sure? It's shopping, Jon."

He winked agreeably. "I know it's shopping. The question is, do you have the patience to help me with the list I've got tucked in my back pocket?"

She smiled. "Only if you have the patience to help me."

"What do you have to buy?" They stepped out onto the bright brick stoop.

"Everything, but I'll be content if I can just find some toys for my sister's youngest boy."

"Now, that's my kind of shopping."

The subway transit system was far more practical than driving a car into the congested city, and so they took the "T" from Cambridge across the river into Boston.

"We must be out of our minds," Angela complained, emerging from the subterranean dankness of the T-stop. Ahead of them the area seemed a near-solid mass of shoppers. "Ten days before Christmas, and we decide to do Faneuil Hall."

Jon gripped her mittened hand firmly in his. "Think of it as an adventure."

The Faneuil Hall marketplace, a collection of warehouselike buildings flanking the colonial assembly hall that lent the area its name, had been the center of Boston commerce for more than a century. Refurbished in the 1970s, it was now home to dozens of trendy shops and restaurants.

It was noon when they arrived, and the tantalizing aromas wafting from the main colonnade drew them in. They squeezed their way through the tight, slow-moving crowd, looking over the various temptations offered by the food vendors.

"Mmm. Everything looks and smells so good!" Angela felt as if her senses were being awakened after a long drugged sleep.

One vendor was grinding exotic coffee beans, another ladling eye-watering chili into paper cups. There were bright healthful fruit salads and irresistibly unhealthful pastries, long crusty breads, Indian curry and Italian gelato. On and on the stalls went, their delicious aromas mingling with the loud buzz of conversation and piped-in Christmas music.

"That." Angela pointed toward an olive-skinned chef spooning falafel into a large Syrian bread pocket. "That looks great."

They shouldered their way to the counter and ordered two. Then, finding only occupied tables in the dining area, they took their food outside. It was a mild day for December, and the sun was radiating warmth off the brick paving of the spacious mall. They found a bench in the middle of the cheerful holiday mayhem, then sat and unwrapped their food.

White fairy lights, twined in the bare trees, sparkled almost unnoticeably in the noonday sun. A block away, a magician was pulling doves from his sleeve to the delight of a large crowd, while from the opposite corner a prophet preached the end of the world. Angela was pleased to see he hadn't a single listener. This close to Christmas, she'd gladly choose magic over doom. She bit into her sandwich, stretched her legs and smiled contentedly. Yes, coming to Boston had definitely been a good idea.

"Jon, listen." Angela clutched his arm. They both sat still, ears perked, then swiveled around.

"Bell ringers!" She laughed in surprised delight.

Standing in the main square in front of Fanueil Hall were a group of professional bell ringers dressed in Victorian costume. They were playing "God Rest Ye Merry Gentlemen."

"It's so Christmasy." Angela laughed again. "Oh, Jon, this is too perfect!"

Jon propped his elbow on the back of the bench, braced his chin on his palm and studied her with amusement.

"What?" she asked warily.

His eyes glittered. "Nothing. It's just that you look happy, that's all. It's good to see you smiling again. I haven't seen you doing too much of that lately."

Angela couldn't hold his gaze. Her stomach was suddenly fluttering giddily. She rested her arm on the back of the bench, dropped her chin onto it and listened to the bell ringers.

Jon was right. She *was* happy today, happy in a pure carefree way she hadn't felt in years. And on a wave of honest insight, she realized she'd made this trip for no one but herself. Not for Ivan. Not to revitalize their relationship. She'd come here because *she* had wanted to. She'd missed having this deep and easy companionship in her life. And as infuriating as Jon could be, she had to admit she'd missed *him*, too.

She also realized that with this visit, the nature of their relationship had changed. She had come to him, not vice versa. Until now, he had made all the overtures. Did that mean she'd finally resigned herself to the fact of their friendship? She turned forward, pensive, and resumed eating.

But nothing was resolved. Nothing. They were ignoring all their recent arguments, as well as the problems that had caused those arguments. They were glossing over the fact that they were seriously involved with other people. But most of all, they were ignoring their painful venture into intimacy when they were eighteen. That incident alone should have made friendship impossible now.

Nevertheless, it felt good being here, and though Angela deplored giving in to feelings that had no sensible base, they were all that seemed to matter today.

Jon squeezed his sandwich wrapper into a ball and sent it in a graceful hook shot into a nearby trash barrel. "Ready?"

"Ready," she mumbled around a last mouthful of food. Wadding up her own wrapper, she pitched it toward the same container and let out a most unladylike crow when it actually went in.

That afternoon they shopped, toured the stately assembly hall above the market where the American Revolution had been engineered, played pinball, bought "Cheers" T-shirts and finally walked up over Beacon Hill to the Commons to watch the Christmas lights wink on in the deepening afternoon gray.

Throughout, Angela was aware of something odd happening to her—a sharpening of her senses, a feeling of awakening from a stupor. As she and Jon leaned toward each other, reading the price tag on a sweater for his mother, she became intensely aware of the clean spicy scent of him. As he took her hand in a crowded elevator, she registered the warmth of him, the hardness of his thigh when he pulled her to his side.

Now, walking through the Commons, Jon's vibrantly alive male presence lay so thick in the air she could hardly breathe.

He'd picked up on her reaction, too. She'd bet money on it. He'd become quiet, watchful, his eyes alert with questions whenever he glanced her way—which made her feel even more ridiculous. Bad enough she was having this problem with Jon's physical attractiveness, but to have him know about it . . . !

She was relieved when they finally returned to the elegant brick house off Harvard Square. Not only were Angela's legs ready to give out, but she'd had enough of walking through winter wonderlands with perhaps the most attractive man in Boston.

She helped him set the table and prepare their meal, fresh tortellini from the Italian north end of the city. They talked amiably enough, but she noticed they both ate quickly, avoiding each other's eyes, and as soon as the dishes were cleared, both dashed to their rooms to get ready for the evening.

Angela used the bathroom first, then relinquished it to Jon. While she stood before the dresser mirror applying her makeup, she heard the water running in the shower, and a vision of Jon in there suddenly flashed across her mind. She squeezed her eyes tight, stamping a raccoon ring of fresh mascara under her right eye.

"Drat!" she swore, though actually she was glad to have something to think about other than hot soapy water sluicing down a certain someone's hard muscled chest.

Half an hour later she emerged from her room, determined to ignore the oversensitized condition she'd worked herself into. She was simply having some sort of mixed-up reaction to how well she and Jon were getting along as friends. That was it. Sure. After all, they *had* made love at one time. It was understandable that her reactions now would be muddled and incapable of discerning what was real and current from what merely echoed from the past. She was certain that she'd be able to control the situation now that she understood its roots.

She found Jon in front of a music stand in the parlor, absorbed in a score. Angela paused in the doorway, making no sound to disturb his concentration. Her eyes traveled from his dark hair down to his polished black shoes. She'd heard of men born to wear tuxes, had even met a few, but Jon put all of them to shame.

He finally looked up, his thickly lashed eyes blinking as he emerged from the music before him. As he focused on her, her heart skipped a beat.

"Hi." Jon's slow warm-as-molasses smile made her fidget self-consciously.

She looked down at her simple black shift. It was fairly classic—straight, sleeveless, scoop-necked—but it was stylishly short, a feature that worried her. "Is this okay?"

Jon stood quite still, his eyes the only part of him that seemed capable of movement. They traveled from her hair, which she'd left loose and swinging about her shoulders, down her bare arms, over her black silk stockings to her ankle-strapped heels. He swallowed. "Yes."

"Yes?" That was it?

"Yes. You look very nice." He turned then and hurried to the coat closet.

Inside the lobby of Symphony Hall, Jon handed Angela her ticket—first balcony, front row, center. He drew a deep breath that lifted his shoulders, but it was several seconds before he expelled it. Small worry lines like quotation marks were etched between his brows.

"Well, I'll be seeing you in a couple of hours. I'm sorry you have to sit alone."

"I'm a big girl."

He coughed and shuffled his feet. "Okay, well . . ."

She couldn't help laughing as an improbable thought struck her. "Stoddard, are you nervous?"

He looked away, over the people mounting the broad marble steps, and tried to shake his head. It came out a tight confused jerk.

"Well, well! This is a first. I wish I had my camera."

Smiling sheepishly, Jon ducked his head. "It isn't funny."

"Of course it isn't." Still chuckling, Angela wrapped her arms around Jon's broad shoulders and hugged him to her. "You know you'll be brilliant. You always are. So, go have fun." Then she kissed his smooth-shaven cheek.

Almost immediately, she realized her mistake. She'd only meant the kiss as a gesture of comfort and support, but suddenly the nearness of him, the scent and heat and hardness of him, were making her knees weak. She gulped, glanced up into his eyes and noticed that the questions that had seemed to plague him earlier had returned. She tried to back off but discovered she couldn't. His hands, pressed against her shoulder blades, seemed frozen into place. For long moments they stared at each other, their lips just inches apart, hearts thudding like kettledrums.

Then, ever so reluctantly, Jon let her go. "Thanks, Angel." He cleared his throat, looking away. "Meet me down in the musicians' lounge when it's over, okay?"

"Will do," Angela called, hurrying off on legs that threatened to give out.

The first part of the program was a cello concerto featuring a guest artist. The performance was wonderful, but Angela was impatient to hear the second half. When the conductor returned to his podium after intermission, Angela was nearly beside herself with anticipation. She'd fully intended to keep her eyes on the maestro tonight, to feel the music through his perspective, but from the very first stroke of his baton, she realized her attention was elsewhere—there, in the horn section.

The symphony began, and unexpectedly Angela felt her eyes stinging, her stomach fluttering again. She usually didn't respond so emotionally at concerts, but tonight it seemed that all her objectivity was stripped away. She was forever poised on the edge of tears, her throat tight, her lips working for control.

It wasn't just the quality of the performance that was getting to her. It wasn't even the music itself. It was seeing Jon down there. Her pride in him was almost too much to bear.

All too soon the piece drew to an end. Angela caught her breath on a sob, and while everyone else got to their feet and applauded, she remained seated, tears streaming down her cheeks. She couldn't have explained her reaction if her life had depended on it.

Finally she gripped the rail before her and staggered to her feet. At the same time, Jon looked up from the stage. She couldn't fathom how he found her so fast, but he did. Given the poor lighting and the distance separating them, she *felt* his gaze more than anything—a direct steady burn that almost physically connected them. Her heart beat wildly. Dear God, she prayed, what was happening here?

She hurried to the nearest ladies' room as soon as possible. Her cheeks were afire and her eyes shone too brightly. She wet a paper towel with cold water and pressed it to her face. She had to get a grip on herself. She was letting her imagination run wild. *Nothing* was happening. She *wasn't* feeling what she thought she was feeling, and Jon definitely was not feeling it in return. They were just friends, and friends put things like physical attractiveness into proper perspective.

Nevertheless, when Angela was walking down the stairs to the musicians' lounge, she realized her stomach was still jumping. And when she spotted Jon walking toward her in his easy long-legged amble, undoing his bow tie, unbuttoning his collar and flashing her one of his knee-buckling grins, she realized that keeping perspective was going to be the hardest job she'd ever tackled.

CHAPTER SEVEN

ANGELA STEPPED OUT to the brick stoop and squinted against the sharp morning light. "Sorry I was such poor company last night. I was more tired than I realized." She didn't meet Jon's eyes. If anything, she'd been overstimulated after the concert, but fearing that her emotions were becoming far too transparent, she'd feigned exhaustion and retreated to her room as soon as they'd come in.

But she hadn't slept much. Perhaps it was the strange bed that had kept her awake, or the symphony that still played through her mind. But more than likely, it was Jon; Jon moving quietly just beyond her door, Jon turning book pages on the other side of the wall—and all the possibilities that lay within the night.

Which was ridiculous, she'd reminded herself with each tormented toss of her body. It couldn't be happening again, it couldn't. The physical attraction she'd felt for him had happened light-years ago. Surely nothing remained of those feelings now. She'd suffered too much as a consequence, learned too well how grievous a mistake it was to cross the line from friendship into intimacy.

Eventually she'd drifted into sleep, and when she'd awakened, she'd felt a renewed conviction that the only sparks flying between her and Jon were in her imagination. She'd joined him for breakfast, firmly resolved to normalize her behavior and return their friendship to firmer footing.

So far, she seemed to be succeeding. But she didn't want to press her luck, and while it was only nine-fifteen, she thought it best to be on her way.

"Are you sure you can't stay longer?" Jon carried her bag down the steps and set it on the walk beside her car.

"Positive. I have a horrid week ahead of me—exams to grade, the college concert Tuesday night, my interview with the WSO board on Thursday..."

Jon's expression sharpened. "That right? I had mine ages ago."

Angela's pulse abruptly leapt. "You...you went through with your interview?"

"Mmm. About a month ago. I'm surprised they scheduled you so late."

Angela said nothing, consumed as she was by the depressing realization that Jon had been interviewed—before he'd found out that she was interested in the directorship, too. That meant he'd given it his best shot. A small moan escaped her throat.

"Hey, no need to worry. They don't have any trick questions up their sleeves. I doubt they could think up any if they tried."

Angela peered up into his lean confident face. "Jon, are you sure you don't want to tell me if you're still in the race?"

He threw back his head and laughed. "Not on your life."

Angela felt a distinct urge to do him bodily harm. Instead, she just glowered.

"Relax, Westgate." He hung his hands over her shoulders, his onyx eyes moving from her hair, along the smooth curve of her cheek to her lips.

And suddenly it was happening again, Angela realized with mounting dread—that mutual awareness arcing between them like a high voltage line. Jon dropped his hands and stepped back awkwardly.

"It's a pity you can't stay longer." He pushed his hand through his hair. "I'm on vacation for the next two weeks, so you wouldn't be putting me out."

Angela moved to her car, quickly opened the door and slid in her bag. "Vacation? How come?" She knew she was blushing.

"The Pops take over, now through Christmas."

"Oh. That's good—I guess." She was feeling rather disoriented again and wished she was on her way.

"Yes, it is. I'm looking forward to the rest."

"Well, Jon, this was fun."

"Mmm. We'll have to do it again sometime."

"Yes. Maybe Cynthia and Ivan will be free to join us then." Angela stole a wary peek at his face. They were both mouthing polite but empty phrases, trying to cover that uncomfortable moment.

"Will you be at WSO rehearsal Wednesday?" she asked, slipping behind the wheel.

"I was planning on it. Would you care to meet up beforehand like we did last week?"

Angela didn't answer right away. Meeting up with him last rehearsal had landed her with a kitchen full of balloons, her determination to remain angry with him destroyed, him sleeping over and Ivan in a lather.

"On second thought," Jon said as if his mind had been running along a similar track, "let's play it by ear. As you say, it's a rough week for you, and frankly, I'm not sure where I'll be Wednesday."

They both knew it was a vague excuse, but it succeeded in getting them off the hook. They smiled, relieved.

"Drive carefully."

"Always do."

"Ha!"

"Ha, yourself. Only one of us got an A in driver education, and it wasn't you." Smiling warmly, she waved and pulled away from the curb.

But once she rounded the corner, her smile wilted. She couldn't be sure what Jon had been feeling back there, but as for herself—Angela groaned aloud—she was in one hell of a mess.

"DAMN!" ANGELA'S Christmas tree listed so far to the left it threatened to topple. This was her first attempt at setting up a tree by herself.

She brushed aside her momentary melancholy and made another stab at adjusting the stand. But when she stepped back, the tree was listing more than ever.

"I give up," she muttered, deciding she'd just have to wait until someone dropped by.

She picked up her half-eaten meat loaf sandwich and took a bite. A sudden thump on her front door nearly made her choke. "Ivan," she whispered. He never used the bell.

Before she could even swallow the bite of sandwich he banged again.

"Coming, coming." She hurried across the room, peered through the window and unlocked the door. "Hi, there."

Ivan walked in, jaw set hard. "So, you're finally home."

Angela clutched her arms against the cold that came in with him. "Yes. Did you go in to school today? I didn't see you."

"You couldn't have looked very hard. Yes, I was there."

Trying to set up her tree alone had deflated most of the Christmas spirit she'd brought home with her from college today. Ivan's attitude now finished off the job.

"What did you do this weekend, Angela?"

Her nerves pulled taut. " Oh, all sorts of things." She smiled forcibly. "I went Christmas shopping, bought a tree." Her smile drooped under his cold stare. "W-what did you do?"

"Does it matter? Do you actually care?"

Angela threaded her fingers together and wrung them like a dishcloth. "Of course I care."

Ivan took a step toward her, planting his fists on his hips. "Where were you Saturday night?"

Angela's brain felt fevered. Ivan's irrational jealousy was the reason they'd argued in the first place. How could she now say she'd spent half the weekend with another man?

"D-did you call me? I thought the plan was we weren't going to have any contact."

Ivan's complexion darkened. "Plan? Seems to me the only person making plans around here is you."

"But . . . it was only an attempt to improve our relationship. Sometimes people who are together too much need a little space."

He pinned her with a derisive stare. "Where were you, Angela?"

"I . . . I . . ."

Ivan's lips curled. "You were with Stoddard, weren't you?"

"I . . ."

"Weren't you?"

Suddenly, Angela had had enough of his bullying. "And what if I was?"

Ivan's fist came down against the sofa. "I knew it!"

Angela's head snapped back with the vehemence of his response.

"Angela, this has got to stop, right here, right now." His pounding fist accented each phrase.

Angela had seen Ivan in a variety of unattractive moods lately, but this anger was something new. Yet it all fit a pattern, a pattern that turned her blood to ice. On legs that threatened to give out, she marched to the door. "I think you'd better leave."

"Not until we settle this."

"We have." She jerked open the door. "I'm tired of your possessiveness, Ivan. I'm tired of a lot of things. Now get out of my house and don't bother coming back. Ever."

His eyes grew fiery. "You're breaking up with me?"

"That's right. Now go." Not knowing where she got the courage, she stepped around him and shoved with all her strength, then slammed the door and turned the lock.

For long minutes afterward, she barely breathed, leaning against the door, knowing he was still out there on the front step. Sweat trickled down her sides. But finally she heard footfalls crunching down the snowy walk and, moments later, his car starting.

She slid down the door, shaking with delayed reaction, and sat on the floor, clutching her head in her hands. Dear Lord, what had happened to her life? It used to be so calm and ordered.

She lifted her gaze to the ceiling, blinking against the stinging in her eyes. Jon was back, Mr. Chaos incarnate—that was what had happened. Unfortunately, at this particular moment, she wished with all her heart that he were here.

She took a deep breath and expelled it slowly. Should she call?

She squinched her eyes tight. No, she'd better not. After the physical awareness she'd felt crackling between them this weekend, the last thing she wanted was for Jon to know she and Ivan had broken up. He'd probably misconstrue her unhappiness as a desire to rekindle a nine-year-old ember. And even if Jon didn't misconstrue her motives, even if those moments of sensual awareness *had* been only figments of her imagination, she still felt disinclined to admit to Jon that her life wasn't perfect.

She didn't know why that bothered her so much. Pride? Was that it? She bobbed her head in a somber rhythm. Yeah, probably, considering how deeply Jon had hurt her nine years ago. The need to prove she'd survived him—and thrived—burned in her like a hard white flame.

Angela hauled herself off the floor, brushed the pine needles from her skirt and headed for the kitchen to put on water for tea. As she puttered, the reality began to sink in: she was free of Ivan.

"Eye-vin," she said aloud. "His name is Eye-vin, not Ee-von, the pretentious jerk!" And that was what she was going to call him from now on.

Angela leaned on the counter, dropping a tea bag into an empty cup, trying to figure out how she'd let herself get involved with such a bozo. But of course she hadn't always seen him in that light. When they'd first started dating, he seemed to possess all the traits she wanted in a man. He'd seemed so mature, so steady and solid, so content with domesticity. With a small wry smile, she realized Ivan had appeared to be everything Jon wasn't, and she wondered if she'd gravitated toward him for precisely that reason.

Hearing the water boil, she pushed herself away from the counter. She prepared her tea, then took the steaming cup over to the patio doors.

As time passed, however, Angela came to realize that Ivan wasn't just solid, didn't just enjoy domestic life. He was practically inert. He did nothing of interest, went nowhere, and he apparently wanted her to do the same. It was almost as if he felt threatened by her activities and the people she came in contact with. Funny—in the beginning, she'd been flattered by how fervently he'd wanted and pursued her. Now she felt suffocated.

How could I have been so stupid? she asked her dim reflection. Jon figured him out, first time they met.

The glass pane was cold against her forehead. Outside the sky had lowered, heavy and gunmetal gray. Such short dark days this time of year. She shivered.

To give herself some credit, she'd started seeing Ivan at one of the lowest ebbs in her life. He'd been there offering her security and companionship for the rest of her days. She supposed it was only natural for her to lean on him.

But he wasn't strong and secure. Ivan was a bully, a weak scared bully, and she was relieved she was finally free of him.

But that was going to be something she kept to herself, at least for a while, she decided. She still needed a protective wedge between her and a certain someone down in Boston.

A smile tugged at the corners of her mouth. Lord, how she wished Jon was here. If anyone knew how to pull her out of the doldrums, it was Jon. She turned and stared at the phone. Maybe it wouldn't do any harm to call. After all, they hadn't really settled the matter of next Wednesday's rehearsal yet....

With her spirits already lifting, Angela set down her cup, flicked on the light switch, chasing the winter gloom, and reached for the phone.

ON WEDNESDAY, Angela opened her front door to find Jon standing there, holding a large ornamental brass horn decorated with holly and a red bow.

"It's very nice, Jon, but I don't think Mr. Beech will allow it."

He smirked. "Very funny."

"It isn't for me, is it? I've already got a wreath."

"No. This is for my door. Come help me hang it."

"I will not. We've got rehearsal in three hours. Come inside. You're letting out all the heat."

Jon strode in, charging the air as he always did with his presence. "Nice tree, Westgate. Going for the natural look this year, I see."

"Oh, that." She cast the still-tipsy tree a pitying look. "I just haven't had time to decorate it yet."

Angela was beginning to feel light-headed. She'd been fighting the condition all day, and she'd succeeded somewhat while still at school. But during this past hour, waiting for Jon to arrive, she'd grown positively flappy. She'd found herself putting milk in the china cupboard, forgetting her purpose when she walked into a room and, like a breathless adolescent, agonizing over which sweater to wear with what jeans.

It wasn't a good situation, and she was beginning to wonder what had ever possessed her to call and invite Jon to dinner. Had she actually believed that the attraction she'd felt during her weekend visit would simply disappear? It hadn't, and although Jon had no idea that she and Ivan had broken up, she still felt terribly open and defenseless in his company, her vulnerability as evident as the blush on her cheek.

"Hanging this won't take long, Angel," Jon said, laying the horn on the table by the door. "We only have to drive a couple of miles."

Angela scowled. "What are you talking about?"

He rocked back on his heels, fingers tucked into the front pockets of his snug jeans. "Are you ready for this? I've put a binder on the Thurgood house."

Angela's jaw dropped. "You're out of your mind."

At times, Jon's grin could turn so gleefully wicked she wanted to shake him. This was one of those times.

"Jon! What are you going to do with a five-bedroom house that's an hour away from Boston?"

"Live in it, I hope."

Angela sank into the nearest chair, her heart doing flip-flops. "I know your mind doesn't work like normal people's, Jon, but this . . . this has got to be the most harebrained, illogical . . . You can't buy a house just like that. Especially not that house."

He laughed, falling onto the sofa opposite her. "All our lives you've been saying, 'Jon, you can't do that,'" he mimicked.

Angela glared at him. She probably had. But just as consistently, he'd always replied, "Just watch me."

"But the cost . . ." she protested.

Jon shrugged negligently.

"The repairs. The size of the place. It's totally impractical."

"But I love that house, Angel."

"So? Does that mean you have to have it?"

He nodded without apology.

"You brat. You're spoiled so rotten a vulture wouldn't have anything to do with you."

Jon stood up and hauled her out of her chair. "Stop grousing and put on your coat."

Still flabbergasted, Angela rode with him to Elm Street and helped him hang the festive horn. It complemented the house's English architecture perfectly.

"Much better." Jon stood back and admired the door with a proprietorial glint in his eyes. Out on the lawn, the For Sale sign was now covered with a Sale Pending banner.

"Jon, it isn't even your house yet. You have no legal right..."

He turned to frown at her, exasperated. "Really, Angel, who cares?"

She shook her head, equally exasperated.

"Besides, it *will* be mine in a few weeks, once I get a mortgage." As he spoke, he pulled a set of keys from his jacket pocket and inserted one of them in the lock.

Angela's eyes widened into horrified saucers. "Jonathan! What are you doing? We could get arrested for trespassing."

He winked devilishly as the heavy door swung in.

The house was even more gracious than she remembered. Angela walked from one high-ceilinged room to another, fighting hard against her mounting excitement. By the time they'd climbed the dark carved staircase and reached the master bedroom, she knew she'd lost the battle. "Oh, Jon, this place is heaven."

Jon planted his elbow on the fireplace mantel and, taking a slow pleased survey of the room, smiled. "Isn't it just!"

"And you really plan to live here? You're moving back to Winston?" She swung toward a window, pretending interest in the view, but she feared Jon had already noticed the moisture gathering in her eyes.

"Yes. I've really missed the place, Angel."

She squared her shoulders and turned to face him. "You do realize how much work you have ahead of you. Everything's going to need repair."

"True. But it's surface work—scrubbing, painting, papering."

Suddenly Angela was overcome by the magnitude of what Jon was doing, so spontaneously, so without care. What a difference between him and Ivan, she thought. Where Ivan was as predictable as a block of cement, Jon was pure mercury.

But on the way downstairs, she grew pensive, because it began to hit her that maybe Jon wasn't as careless as she thought.

"How does Cynthia like the house?" she somehow got out over the jealousy clotting in her throat.

"Oh, she doesn't know about it yet. She's not coming home from her assignment till tomorrow. I'm supposed to pick her up at the airport."

Angela was glad her back was to Jon, because she was sure her expression was pained. Was he thinking of marrying Cynthia? Is that why he wanted to buy this big family house? Was he looking forward to filling it with a brood of little Stoddards? Angela's stomach cramped. And why Winston? Why the very street where they'd grown up? Did he expect her to come visit them in the future? Hadn't he done enough, or was he planning to make hurting her a lifetime pursuit?

"Before we leave, you've got to see the backyard, Angel." Jon fit his long fingers around her arm just above the elbow, hardly denting the thick sleeve of her white wool coat. Yet his touch, light as it was, still sent shivers racing through her.

He opened the kitchen door and led her out to a flagstoned patio strewn with wet leaves. Before them, a half acre of lawn, vine-tangled rose arbors, gardens and bare trees were shrouded in gray winter light.

"Lots of potential here," Angela commented, wondering if Cynthia liked to garden. She felt her mouth quiver and looked aside before adding, "I wish you all the best, Jon."

He gazed down at her, clasped the back of her neck and squeezed. It was a gesture anyone would recognize as merely friendly. But when he should have let go, his hand remained there, fingers tracing a shivery path up into her hair. Her pulse thumped, louder, faster. She tried not to misconstrue his intentions, but, Lord, he had to know what he was doing. Quickly she stepped away, molding her expression into as blank a mask as she could muster. "We'd better be heading back. I have to put our dinner in the oven."

He nodded, and the uncomfortable moment was dispelled. "Maybe we'll even have time to do something about that poor tree of yours."

Twenty minutes later, Jon was on his hands and knees, reaching for the tree stand. "You hold. I'll loosen."

Angela sighed unenthusiastically, reaching through the branches to grip the sticky trunk. "This isn't necessary, you know. The tree's fine as it is. I'm getting kind of fond of it, actually."

"Sweetheart, sweetheart, where's your Christmas spirit?"

"Out partying in somebody else's life, I think."

Jon made a small tsk-tsk of disapproval, and Angela cast a quick glance down at his crouched form, ready to tsk right back. But the next moment, she forgot her intention and became totally mesmerized by the strong curve of his back, the taut lines of his thighs, the crescent of still-tanned skin above his leather belt where his sweater had ridden up.

"What time's your interview tomorrow?"

Angela wrenched her gaze away guiltily. "Um... four."

"Are you ready for it?"

"Yes. Maybe." Actually, she'd been hoping to prepare today.

"Can you lift? I want to turn the stand so the screws won't sink into the same cockeyed holes you made."

She was glad Jon was oblivious to the nonsense that had been running through her mind. She didn't understand it herself, and Lord only knew what he would make of it.

Jon finally got to his feet and gave the tree a satisfied nod. "Much better. Now, where are the lights?"

With Jon's help, Angela spent the next hour stringing the old multicolored lights she'd known since she was a child, hanging the fragile glass balls that had traveled down the decades—and trying not to pay attention to their steadily growing mutual awareness.

Or was the problem just hers? After all, it was her fingers that fumbled with ornaments, her cheeks that flared at his slightest glance. Unfortunately he quickly became aware of her awareness, which only compounded the problem. He grew quietly constrained, moving as if he wanted to avoid touching her, and twice when she peeked through the branches, she was startled to find him peeking back, his brow puckered. The day was definitely taking on an uncomfortable feel.

"Dinner break," she announced as the oven buzzer sounded.

"Hold it, Westgate. You've got a branch stuck in your hair."

"A branch?"

"Well, twiggy things. Tip your head."

She did, and Jon worked his long fingers through her hair, the soap-and-cinnamon warmth of his body wrapping her in an intoxicating spell. She shivered under his gentle ministrations.

"Did I pull?"

She shook her head.

"Okay. It's out."

"Thanks." She didn't dare meet his eyes, but hurried off to the kitchen, instead. There she braced herself on the counter, hands splayed, and pulled in a steadying breath. She had to get hold of herself. It would be too humiliating if Jon guessed the effect he was having on her.

"Is there anything I can do to help?"

She swung around to find him watching her. "Uh, no. Table's all set. Well, yes. Here." She bumped awkwardly into a chair as she handed him the salad bowl.

She noted his confusion, then realized he was staring at the small kitchen table. "No, the table in the dining room." She pressed a dimmer switch, and a small chandelier brought the adjacent room to life. She saw Jon's eyes widen, saw him swallow.

"Somebody sure went to a lot of trouble."

Angela's cheeks blazed. She'd set the table before his arrival, deciding on a whim to use her grandmother's china, the Waterford crystal, linen napkins and tall white candles.

"What's the occasion?" Jon's voice was thick with apprehension.

She bit her lip, mortified. "Nothing. I just don't get to use my nice things too often."

He nodded guardedly, setting down the salad bowl. She handed him a bottle of wine and corkscrew, and hurried back to the kitchen. When she returned with the serving cart, he was pouring. In tense silence, she set out the chicken cordon bleu, rice pilaf and green beans with almonds, while Jon lit the candles. By the time they sat, she doubted she'd be able to swallow a single bite.

In all the years she'd known Jon, never had they gone through anything quite as uncomfortable as this. And the worst part was, she didn't even understand what *this* was.

"What are your plans for Christmas?" He cut into his chicken with a vigor more likely born of stress than of hunger.

Angela watched him chew, watched him swallow, wipe his mouth, sip his wine. She studied his long capable hands shifting utensils, noticed the candlelight flickering in his deep midnight eyes—all before remembering to answer him.

"I'm going to Peg's for dinner."

"You and Ivan?"

"No, Ivan won't be go—" Grabbing up her wine goblet, she took a swallow. She considered telling Jon the truth—that she and Ivan were kaput, and if he wanted her, she was his for the asking. All he had to do was crook his finger, give her one of his killer grins, and she'd be at his feet.

Oh, Lord, what was she thinking? She glanced across the candlelight to find Jon watching her, his dark head tilted, his curious gaze taking in her every facial tick and hand jitter.

"Ivan's . . . going to visit his mother in Cleveland." Cleveland? She popped a forkful of rice into her mouth and fell into a spell of coughing. Ivan's mother had passed away five years ago. "What are your plans?" she asked hastily.

"I'm flying down to Florida Christmas Day to be with my parents. My flight leaves around noon."

"Is Cynthia going, too?"

He was quiet an unusually long time before replying, "No."

They resumed eating, but questions lay so thick in the air she thought she would suffocate. Finally Jon looked up from his food.

"Cynthia and I . . . we're not as tight as you seem to think."

Angela's heart lurched.

"In fact, we've just about stopped dating." He tucked into his food again, grimacing as if he regretted this admission. Her silence eventually drew his attention. "What? Why are you smiling?"

She tried to wipe the expression from her face. "This is a crazy world. If you want to know the truth, Ivan and I aren't an item anymore, either."

A dozen expressions shifted in his eyes. "Oh, I'm sorry."

She accepted his condolence with a solemn nod.

"This *is* a crazy world." Jon seemed to be fighting off a smile, too. "So, it looks like we're both at loose ends this Christmas, doesn't it?"

"Looks like." Her breath had stalled somewhere in her throat.

Suddenly he leaned forward, face alight. "Angel, let's do it."

Her eyes snapped up. "Do what?"

"The climb. Remember our dream of camping out in the White Mountains on Christmas Eve?"

She lowered her knife and fork very carefully. Of course she remembered. The plan was they'd take their instruments with them, and as the sun rose on Christmas morning, they'd play a few carols. At sixteen, she'd thought the idea wonderful, the height of romance. But at twenty-seven, she saw it for what it was—pure adolescent folly. "You can't be serious."

"As an undertaker."

"But you've got a plane to catch and I . . ."

"We'll be off the mountain in plenty of time. Really, Angel, it's something we should do before we get too old. Some dreams shouldn't be put off."

"I'm afraid this one already has been."

"Don't say that. It's bound to be one the most moving experiences of your life, a moment out of time." His voice swelled with mock eloquence. "A direct communication with the sublime and transcendent. Besides, what else are you going to do Christmas Eve without a man in your life?"

Her look was dry. "Be warm. Be safe."

"*Rrkktt!*" Jon made a tight creaking noise deep in his throat, hunched his shoulders and contorted his hands.

"What are you doing?"

"An imitation. Of you—atrophying."

Laughing in spite of herself, Angela whipped her napkin across the table. He caught it in one deft hand and tossed it back.

"I'm going," he said with finality. "I wish you'd come along. It was *our* dream, not just mine."

"Was not. This is stamped with Stoddard eccentricity through and through." She paused. "You're really going?"

"Yes."

"Alone?"

"Apparently."

"You shouldn't. It's dangerous."

He leaned on his hand and cocked one dark eyebrow in a most enticing invitation. Angela was sure her toes curled.

Finally she threw up her hands. "All right! I'll go. But mark my words, Jon, it won't be what you think. All it's going to be is cold."

She picked up her fork and tried to resume eating. What had she just agreed to? Hike with Jon into the very mountains where they'd become lovers. Granted, it would be too cold this time to do anything but struggle to survive. Still, thoughts were bound to arise. As they were now.

Angela peered up warily. Jon was staring at his plate, his face gone serious. Her heart bumped wildly against her rib cage. Did he ever think back on that night nine summers ago, as she so often did? Did his blood stir, even a little, at the memory of their youthful passion? Is that what was giving him such serious pause right now?

His gaze lifted, and for one raw second she knew the answer. At this moment they were both back there, lying in a tent, locked in each other's arms, utterly lost in each other's eyes.

Jon cleared his throat, glanced away, turned back again. He seemed to be searching for something to say or do to rescue them from the moment. "Angel, look." He smiled and, linking his thumbs, positioned his hands near one of the candles, casting a shadow onto the wall—a bird, she surmised.

"Cute."

"Nothing compared to my rabbit."

But he didn't do a rabbit, and neither of them smiled. Jon dropped his head to his hands, burying his splayed fingers in his hair in a gesture of undisguised desperation.

"Help me out, Angel," he groaned. "I don't know how to handle it, either."

She froze, every inch of her instantly awake and pulsing. Was it possible? Had Jon been battling an attraction toward her, too? Is that why he'd been so quietly reserved?

She leapt to her feet and began to clear the table. Maybe if she got busy, they could let his comment pass. Obviously, he didn't welcome the attraction anymore than she did.

"Let me help."

"Sure." Her response was falsely bright.

For the next few minutes, the room was filled with such a clatter they might have been clearing tables in a major restaurant, instead of a simple dinner for two. Angela had no idea if busyness was helping him, but it was doing nothing for her. The faster she moved, the more aware of him she grew.

She was about to remove the breadbasket when Jon reached for it, too. Their eyes met, and in that one shattering look, she knew it was all over. Jon yanked the basket from her limp fingers, hurled it across the room, sending rolls bouncing off the walls and pictures, and caught her up in his arms.

"I've come to a decision," he announced. "This is how we should handle it." And the next moment he was kissing her.

He felt even better than she'd imagined. Far, far better. Suddenly a floodgate of restraint seemed to break, unleashing a torrent of desire too long pent up.

"Oh, Lord, Angel!" Jon came up for air with a gasp. She ran her fingers up his neck, sinking them into his luxuriant dark hair, hair she'd been longing to touch since forever. He dipped his head again, eyes closing, and brushed his open mouth over hers. Their breath mingled in a disbelieving sigh.

Was this really happening? she wondered, reeling in a happiness so profound it frightened her. "Jon?" The word was a tremulous whisper.

He opened his eyes, a languid sweep of black lashes. "Shh," he admonished, moving in to kiss her again. She didn't protest. Kissing him felt too good, too much like coming home. It was what she'd been burning to do all afternoon, and the miracle of the situation was he'd apparently been feeling the very same way.

As the first desperate moments passed, Jon's embrace relaxed, and he became more sensually aware of her, easing into slow, deep, lingering kisses that made her melt against him. He pressed his hands down her back, fitting her soft curves to every hard plane of him, and when she thought she couldn't get any closer, his hands slid into the back pockets of her jeans and pressed her closer still. The intimacy almost buckled her knees.

From what seemed a long distance away, a clock chimed its quarter-hour melody. With his mouth still moving over hers, Jon turned in the direction of the clock. Reluctantly he lifted his head.

"Time to go." Even his whisper sent curls of heat through her stomach.

Oh, this was truly a terrible situation! She'd known she was feeling a pull toward him, but the volatility and force of her response was something she couldn't have anticipated in a million years.

"Jon..." She touched his moist lips with fingers that trembled. He kissed them, took one between his teeth. "Jon, this can't happen."

But instead of sharing her trepidation, he only grinned. "Angel, babe, I think it already has."

CHAPTER EIGHT

REHEARSAL THAT EVENING passed in a blur. Angela remembered so little of it that, leaving the theater, she decided she must have spent the entire time out of body. What a dreadful dilemma she and Jon had created in a few short minutes of runaway passion.

"Well, Jon, I guess I won't be seeing you again until the concert." She tried to modulate her voice and pretend she was saying good-night to just any colleague.

Jon let the theater door fall shut behind them and gripped her arm tight. "Let's go for a walk." His face was grim.

With a pulse beating frantically at the base of her throat, Angela looked toward her car, parked across the street behind his. She'd suggested they come in separate vehicles to eliminate the necessity of his going back to her place. But all along she'd known they couldn't just walk away from what had happened.

They locked their instruments in their respective cars, then started toward the lighted windows of the downtown shops. Everything was closed at this hour, sidewalks deserted, garlands and Christmas lights swaying forlornly in a fine mist.

"Jon, I'm sorry." Angela had been rehearsing the words all evening, and now they poured out almost of their own volition. "I hope you can forget what happened back at my place. It was a mistake—I think we both know that—and I'd like to pretend it never happened."

Jon's footsteps slowed. "But it did happen, Angel, and it's not going to go away, no more than what happened nine years ago has gone away. We're going to have to face it sooner or later."

She closed her eyes tight. "No."

"But aren't you at all curious about it? Where it's coming from? Where it's going?"

"I know where it's going," she lashed back. "That's what I'm trying to head off. I don't want that to ever happen again."

Jon's left eyebrow lifted in an ironic curve. "Sorry it was such an unpleasant experience for you."

Angela's face reddened.

"What are you afraid of?"

"Don't be obtuse, Jon. You know as well as I what happened to our friendship the last time we . . . the last time."

Jon paused at a storefront window, staring with unfocused eyes at a mannequin dressed in holiday glitter. He rubbed his gloved hand along his jaw. "I've been thinking . . ." He spoke slowly, cautiously. "Maybe we'll be able to handle it now that we're older."

Angela glared at his profile, hardly able to believe his gall. For whatever mysterious reason, she aroused a physical need in him, and simply because he had that need, he assumed he had the right to satisfy it—like a child, suffering no thoughts of consequences, looking no further than the moment.

"Maybe you can handle it, but I'm not that sophisticated."

His brow knit. "I'm not sure I understood your objections."

No, he wouldn't. To him their lovemaking had been nothing more than a physical encounter, and apparently not a very important one at that. He hadn't shared any of her emotional turmoil, didn't have a clue how deep her heartache had run when she'd seen him just days later with another girl. Jon was a sensitive person in many ways, but when it came to sex and love, he was a moron.

"Let me put it this way, Jon. You've never been serious about a girl in your life, not for any length of time, anyway." They resumed walking. "I have a few theories why that's so."

"I'm sure you do." His sardonic tone made her hesitate. "Oh, please, don't let me stop you."

"Well, I have a hunch it's because you're afraid of serious relationships." She paused again.

"Go on," he prodded.

"You're afraid your career will bog down and you won't reach your potential. It's that, or else you just love the chase and get bored once you've made your conquest." She swallowed with difficulty. "So over the years they've come and they've gone, an endless parade of knockouts. But through them all, I remained because I was different. I was special to you, and by some stroke of dubious luck, we seem to have regained a measure of that closeness. And...and I think I like it. So you'll just have to understand when I say I don't want to be your girlfriend, Jon. I don't want to be...trivialized."

"Trivialized? You think I'd trivialize you?"

"Most definitely. I'd be put in a box marked Temporary Diversion, and then we'd have nothing, because after you lost interest, we sure as hell couldn't return to being just friends."

They'd reached the end of the block, crossed the street and headed back on the other side. The mist had thickened, spangling Jon's hair with silver droplets. He trudged along in silence, a frown darkening his handsome features.

"But we're friends now, after being lovers," he retorted.

"Yes, but it took nine years. Next time, I'm afraid forever won't be long enough to heal the breach."

Jon sighed, his lips pressing in defeat. "You're right. You're right. About everything, damn it."

Angela stopped dead. "I am?"

He nodded. "And I sure as hell don't want to lose you again." He tucked his hand under her coat collar, pulled her toward him and kissed the damp crown of her head.

Angela fought against a sudden weakening in her knees. "Wh-what did you say?"

He smiled. "I have a story I should tell you. Maybe it'll help you better understand what I mean. It happened one night about five years ago when I was traveling with that orchestra from Barcelona. We were in Prague at the time, and it was late, after midnight. We'd come in on the train from Rome that afternoon, performed that evening, and I was exhausted. I was turning down the blankets on the dormitory bed I'd been assigned when the guy in the bed next to me asked who I was talking to. I told him nobody, and he laughed. He said being on the road had finally gotten to me, because he'd definitely seen my lips moving.

"Well, I lay awake for a long time that night, and I finally realized I *had* been talking to someone. To you."

"Me?" Heat rose right up to Angela's scalp.

"Uh-huh. I'd been telling you all about the fifteenth-century palace we'd played in and about the food and the countryside. I also realized I'd been doing that for so long, keeping a running dialogue with you in my head, that I wasn't even aware of it anymore. It had become habit. My day wasn't complete until I did. Talking to you gave it order, validity. Do you know what I'm saying?"

The lights strung across the street blurred in the tears that suddenly welled up in Angela's eyes. She nodded.

"And, well, I don't want to mess with anything that important, Angel. I'm still not sure how we're supposed to take back what happened tonight. We had something really hot going there for a while." He grinned down at her briefly, maybe even self-consciously, before becoming serious again. "But if you say we have to, then we have to. As I said, I don't want to lose you again."

They'd come full circle and were back at the theater, its lights extinguished now, doors locked. Angela paused under the street lamp and dared a glance up into Jon's fathomless dark eyes. For all her show of clearheaded logic, she wasn't sure she knew what to do about what had happened, either. How *could* they go on, pretending nothing had changed between them? After those kisses, those embraces—how *did* you take back miracles like those?

But somehow they would have to. Otherwise, she was headed toward more heartache than she knew how to handle.

They crossed the street and while she unlocked her car he asked, "Do you still have your camping gear?"

"Yes." She was relieved that he considered the issue of their attraction closed and had moved on. "I packed it away in the basement of the condo."

"Good. I think my parents still have mine. I'll phone them tomorrow and ask them to ship it express."

Angela chewed on her lip. "Jon, do you really think it's wise for us to go on that hike?" Perhaps the best way to handle the situation between them and preserve their friendship was to spend as little time alone with each other as possible.

"Wise?" He turned from unlocking his car. "What do you mean?" He seemed genuinely unaware of her concern.

"Well, for one thing, it's dumb. And for another, it's dangerous, and I've been having second thoughts. I'd much rather stay home with my tree, maybe bake some cookies and listen to a Bing Crosby Christmas album. If I venture out at all, it'll be to midnight service."

Jon laughed. "Start getting your gear together, Westgate. You know where you're going to be Christmas Eve as well as I do." He folded himself into his car, laughed at her again in the rearview mirror and zoomed away from the curb.

Angela sat there long after he'd left. He was right, damn him. She'd probably follow Jon into the jaws of hell if he asked. What was the matter with her, anyway?

The drizzle had turned to unabashed rain, glittering like shredded cellophane in the bright illumination of the streetlight. She shivered and, wilting over the steering wheel, moaned a misery that rose from deep inside her.

He didn't understand, did he? She'd told him they couldn't pursue this mutual attraction because she didn't want to ruin their friendship, and he'd agreed she was right. But he didn't *really* understand.

Perhaps she should have talked about it. But how? How could she admit that their lovemaking was the most phenomenal experience of her life, an experience she hadn't even tried to duplicate with anyone else? And the deepest embarrassment of all—how could she confess that she'd been head over heels in love with him at the time? What a fool she'd make of herself. She didn't think she could bear his pity or contempt.

Angela turned on the ignition, adjusted the heat, glanced in the mirror—and glanced again. How wide and frightened her eyes appeared—and how clear their message. Yes, she was worried Jon would discover she'd been in love with him in the past. But she was even more afraid he'd discover she loved him *now*.

She shut her eyes tight and winced. She really did love him, didn't she? But then, had she ever stopped?

But he'd spurned her, rejected her in record time, and she didn't have the slightest doubt he'd do it again.

She pulled away from the curb, her chin tilted in defiance. No, there would be no more loving between her and Jon. She'd be his friend, she'd talk to him on the phone, go out for the occasional meal, and, heaven help her, she'd go on his hike. But never again was she going to let him break her heart.

THE WOMEN ON THE BOARD were already gathered around the conference table in the theater office when Angela arrived for her interview the next afternoon. Mr. Beech stood apart, gazing out the window. He turned.

"Good afternoon, Miss Westgate," he said in his usual brusque manner, but his hand drifted to her arm and squeezed in a private gesture of support.

She smiled her appreciation, wishing she were calmer and better prepared. This was the most important interview of her life, but recent events had completely derailed her from her purpose. On a fleeting wave of paranoia, she wondered if Jon had set out to do so on purpose.

Mr. Beech took a seat at the head of the table and motioned for Angela to sit nearby. It was then that she noticed how pale and tired he looked.

"Would you care for some tea, Miss Westgate?" The oldest woman on the board, Mrs. Fitzhugh, loved to entertain and evidently considered an interview excuse enough to cart out bone china and an antique silver service.

"Yes, thank you," Angela replied.

The women were a motley bunch. There was 190-pound Mrs. Conroy in her designer sweats, Mrs. Stevens wearing a Palm Beach tan and a condescending sneer, and Mrs. Estes who was trying to pretend no one knew she'd just returned from the Betty Ford Clinic.

A disparate crew, yet they all were friends, wives of prominent professionals, dedicated to charity and getting their picture in the paper as often as possible.

Mrs. Fitzhugh passed tea all around, and then they opened folders containing copies of Angela's application. For almost two full minutes the room was silent except for the turning of pages. Angela rubbed her damp palms along her thighs and tried to quell her nervousness. She looked at Mr. Beech, but he'd shut his eyes.

"So, tell us about yourself," Mrs. Conroy said, lifting a teacup in her plump white hand. "Why do you think you'd make a good music director with the Winston Symphony?"

Angela wrenched her concerned gaze from Mr. Beech, straightened her spine and plunged in. For the next few minutes, she reminded them of her training and work experience, but what she really tried to emphasize were the duties she'd fulfilled with the WSO.

"I've been with the group for seven years. I know the audience, know what pleases them. But more importantly, I understand the musicians, what they can do—and what they can't. I believe it's terribly important to choose music they can handle comfortably."

Mr. Beech sat forward. "I'd like to add that when they can't handle the music, as is often the case with the less proficient players, Miss Westgate gives most generously of her time to help them. She's been known to have people over to her house for extra practices, and she's a whiz at rewriting music for them, giving them a simplified version that dovetails so well with the original the audience is none the wiser."

"Really?" Mrs. Stevens looked offended, cheated perhaps, and Angela began to think Mr. Beech hadn't done her any favors.

"But what special vision will you bring to the ensemble?" Mrs. Fitzhugh inquired.

"Vision?" Angela blinked. Suddenly she wondered how Jon had answered that question. She could almost see him now, playing the tormented artiste, fulfilling their every warped expectation—and laughing up his sleeve while he did. "I won't be bringing any new vision. This isn't the Boston Symphony." The women exchanged glances.

"What a community ensemble needs," she went on, "is not a visionary but a common-sense, workmanlike teacher, a person who's patient, able to take music apart and present it in understandable, digestible segments. Someone who absolutely loves their work, too, and I'll defy you to find anyone who loves working with the WSO as much as I do."

Defy? Angela cringed. Emotion was getting the best of her. She was being too forceful, phrasing things badly.

Mrs. Stevens lifted her long pointed nose and sniffed. "I do believe you're serious about this application."

"Yes, I'm quite serious." Good Lord, did they think she wasn't? "Why?"

"Well, you must admit, it is a bit unusual for a woman to aspire to the podium."

Angela's fingers curled into her thighs. So, it *was* happening, just as she'd feared. They were ignoring her qualifications and zeroing in on her gender. "I...I can understand why you think that," she answered diplomatically. "In the seventies there were virtually no women conducting. But times have changed. Female conductors have definitely become figures to contend with. There's Marin Alsop, Catherine Comet, Joann Falletta..." She wished she'd brought along a few magazines to support her point.

"But how will you handle such a large group? How do you expect to project authority?"

Angela couldn't believe she was being torpedoed in such a sexist manner by other women. Still, she smiled. "I understand. There's an ingrained image of the conductor as the embodiment of leadership and authority, and traditionally those are qualities that the popular mind has reserved for men. But surely you must understand how the popular mind can change, and *has* changed over the past twenty years."

Angela was far from finished, but Mrs. Conroy interrupted, anyway. "What happens if you someday find yourself in the family way?"

Angela was sure steam was whistling from her ears by now. "Since I'm single, the issue is irrelevant. But just for the record, Gisele Ben-Dur made her debut with the Israel Philharmonic when she was nine months pregnant."

This remark elicited a series of sniggering oh-mys and good-heavenses.

"Miss Westgate, what ever would you wear?" Mrs. Fitzhugh inquired.

This sparked interest all around, except from Mr. Beech who cast her a helpless look of sympathy. Angela suddenly didn't care that she was in the middle of her interview. She leaned across the table and asked, "Are you okay?"

He nodded, fluttering his hand for her to pay no attention to him.

"What did you say, Mrs. Conroy?"

The woman was chuckling. "I asked what you'd wear, dear. The traditional tails?"

Angela fought to keep her smile in place. "I have two outfits that my superiors find quite tasteful. Clothing has never been a concern."

But evidently it was to this group. They wanted to know what the outfits looked like, the material, even their cost.

Angela eventually steered the discussion toward her plans for the future of the WSO—such as a children's concert series and combined productions with the local choral group. She also wanted to discuss new concepts for raising funds, but their faces had gone blank as soon as the discussion veered away from clothing.

Angela left the theater stewing. Conducting the Winston Symphony meant more to her than anything, and the board members hadn't taken her seriously! She slammed the car door and turned the key so hard the ignition ground. They simply hadn't *wanted* to take her seriously.

By the time she got home, however, her anger had plunged to despair. Her first thought was to call Jon. Her second thought was that it was Jon's fault she hadn't been better prepared in the first place, and she'd be hanged before she'd go running to him for sympathy. She should have spent yesterday preparing, anticipating the curves the board might throw her, rehearsing her answers until they sparkled. That was her usual method. Instead, she'd squandered the entire day on Jon. She really ought to have her head examined, she decided as she headed for the bathroom where she'd find consolation in a long hot soak.

But even as she turned on the tap, she knew her anger toward Jon was only an excuse not to call, not to admit that he *could* ease her burdens, *could* make her laugh, an excuse not to face the truth that Jon was very quickly becoming the center of her universe.

THE NEXT AFTERNOON Angela's phone was ringing when she unlocked her door. "Coming, coming ... Hello?"

"Angela, it's Mr. Beech."

She dropped her canvas satchel on the kitchen counter, and Christmas cards, given to her on this, the last day of school before the break, spilled out. "Mr. Beech! How are you?"

"That's why I'm calling. Could you come by the house this afternoon? We have to discuss Sunday's concert."

"Of course. I'll be there right away."

Angela drove across town in record time. She hadn't needed to ask to know that something was wrong.

Mrs. Beech answered the door. She was a tall woman with patrician features and pure white hair pulled into an elegant twist—every inch her husband's counterpart.

"Henry's waiting for you in the study, dear."

Angela caught the woman's arm. "How's he feeling? He didn't look well during my interview yesterday. Did he ...?"

"Have another heart attack? I worried about the same thing myself. I even took him into emergency last night, but the doctor in attendance said Henry was fine. His medication did have to be changed, though, and I must admit he looks better today."

"Thank heaven." Angela followed the woman down the hall. "I won't keep him long."

She found her mentor sitting by the fire, a green tartan blanket tucked up around his chest.

"Angela! Here already?" He laid aside the book he was reading. "Have a seat." He waved a hand toward the chair opposite him.

Angela unbuttoned her coat and perched on the edge of the seat, her eyes brimming with questions.

And he wasted no time in answering. "Angela, I need you to take my place Sunday."

Suddenly the room began to whirl. "What?"

"You're going to have to conduct the Christmas program. I thought I could do it, but . . ." He shook his shaggy white head.

"But the concert is only two days away. I can't!"

The old conductor pierced her with his most formidable look. "Nonsense. You've filled in for me on any number of occasions."

The metallic taste of terror rose in her throat. "Yes, but that was at rehearsal, bits here and there."

Mr. Beech spread his hands on the blanket, old spotted hands that trembled. "Angela, I can't do it." She'd never heard his voice so sad, so defeated.

"Can't you cancel?"

He gazed at the fire. "I could." Again that defeat. "But the Christmas concert is our biggest draw. We'd lose thousands of dollars if I did, and finances being what they are, we'd—" he swallowed "—go under."

"What?"

He nodded grimly. "After sixty-eight years, the WSO would have to fold."

The floor seemed to dissolve beneath Angela's feet. "I didn't know we were doing so badly."

"It's this damned economy." He sat forward, suddenly rigid with bitterness. "Priorities getting all turned around, cuts being made where they shouldn't . . ." As if exhausted by the effort, he sank back into the chair. "But even if money wasn't an issue, think of the musicians, Angela, all the hours they've put in just for the love of it."

Angela felt the corners of her mouth turning downward. And what about all *his* hard work? she thought. This was Mr. Beech's last concert. Is this how he was to be remembered—with a cancel? She closed her eyes, feeling trapped, wanting to cry.

As she did too often these days, she thought unexpectedly of Jon. Of course he wasn't responsible for this particular calamity, but still she found it odd; why didn't calamities of this magnitude happen when he wasn't around?

Jon! Good Lord, she'd be conducting Jon!

"If you won't do it for the good of the organization," Mr. Beech continued, "how about doing it for yourself? This is a golden opportunity to prove to the board exactly what you're made of."

Angela's head snapped up. That was the last thing on her mind. "But I might fall flat on my face and prove they're right. I don't know the score as well as you do...."

"But you could. I'm not going anywhere for the next two days. Are you?"

Staring at her tightly knit fingers, she shook her head.

"Good. So what do you say? Shall we go for the glory?"

Angela groaned in painful insecurity.

"I'll take that for a yes."

Angela stayed with Mr. Beech for the rest of that day, fine-combing the music and listening diligently to his advice. Jon called her that evening, and when she told him what she was up to, the line buzzed with silence.

Then, "You're going to be doing *what* Sunday?"

"Conducting the concert. Oh, and I'm asking everyone to be there at noon for an extra rehearsal."

More silence.

"What's the matter, Jon?" She couldn't help smiling. "Having difficulty with the idea of me on the podium and you in the pit?"

"No, of course not."

"Are you sure? Our roles are usually just the opposite."

"No, it isn't that."

"Then what is it?" Her smile faded. "Oh. I see. You just don't think I can do it."

Jon cleared his throat. "Can you? I mean, it's such short notice."

"Thanks for the vote of confidence, pal."

"It's concern, Angel, concern. I know how wired you get when you don't feel prepared."

"I'll be prepared."

"I have another question." Jon's voice had an edge she couldn't quite define. "Why you?"

Her back straightened. "Why not me? I *am* Mr. Beech's assistant."

"But doesn't it strike you as just a bit unfair to the others who've applied for his job?"

"Like who, Jon?" she asked insinuatingly.

He groaned. "Angel, can we drop this? I've got a headache like you wouldn't believe."

"So, now I give you headaches."

"You got that right. Insomnia and indigestion, too."

"Good." She was relieved to hear him laugh. She hadn't meant to start an argument.

"I don't suppose you'd care to go skiing tomorrow?" he asked.

"The only thing I'm doing from now until Sunday is preparing for the concert."

Jon gave a low growl of frustration. "All right. I'll call tomorrow to see how you're doing. Take care."

As it turned out, Jon called her several times the next day, but Angela cut each of those calls short. During their last conversation he said, "Are you sure you don't want to take a break and go out for a quick bite?"

"Positive." Nothing was going to come between her and her purpose this time, especially not Jon. "I'll see you at the theater tomorrow."

"You don't even want me to come by and pick you up?"

"Uh-uh. I prefer to be alone till it's over."

"This isn't healthy, Angel," he said dryly.

"Wrong. This is how I thrive. You'll see."

She hung up, wiped Jonathan Stoddard from her thoughts, donned her earplugs to shut out distracting noises and once again mounted the makeshift podium before the mirror in her study. Then, raising her baton to cue an imagined orchestra, she proceeded to conduct the next day's program in the concert hall of her mind.

THE THEATER WAS richly draped in laurel garland caught up in deep swags by balsam wreaths. Their fragrance greeted Angela the minute she came in off the street. Two tall fir trees, heavy with decorations, stood on either side of the stage. The floors were unusually clean, the air pleasantly heated, everything about the place saying: this is it, show time.

Angela walked up the center aisle in a haze of unreality. As prepared as she was, her stomach still quivered. She paused halfway to the stage and took a few deep calming breaths. The worst thing she could do was impart her nervousness to the musicians. Given the circumstances, they were going to be skittish enough.

"Good morning." She smiled at five people who'd somehow managed to arrive before her. They returned wary nods. But then she'd expected that and tried not to take their wariness to heart. She hurried backstage and, after hanging her coat, ducked into the washroom to check her appearance.

Although she'd told the board that clothing wasn't an issue with her, this morning she'd dressed with inordinate care.

The results were gratifying. Looking back at her from the mirror was a young woman who projected strength and confidence. She'd elected to wear her black tuxedo today, complete with pleated shirt, white bow tie and cummerbund. But there was no mistaking her femininity, either. The suit was made of an elegant brocade and cut on lines that enhanced her figure. She'd applied her makeup carefully, arranged her hair in a glistening French braid, and finished off the look with pearl-cluster earrings and a lace-edged hanky tucked into her pocket. She smiled at her reflection, noting the nervous but eager excitement in her eyes.

"Yes," she whispered. "Let's do it!"

As she left the washroom, Jon was just hanging his coat.

"Westgate!"

"Hello, Jon." She tried to quell the racing of her heart at the sight of him.

His admiring eyes traveled the length of her, up, down, then up and down again. For once in his life, he seemed speechless.

She beamed. She was definitely ready now. She *would* lead the WSO through this calamity. She *would* prove to the board she deserved the conductor's job. And finally, finally, she would show Jon that she could excel at something, too.

She stood at the podium and scanned the sea of guarded faces before her. Three hours until show time. Three measly hours to prove she could pilot this ship as capably as Mr. Beech.

But damn it all, she was better than Mr. Beech. She had more energy, broader understanding, clearer expression and, if she was really honest, far better rapport with the musicians. She lifted her chin and smiled with dignity and confidence. She loved this group, and for all the panic she'd suffered in the past two days, she absolutely adored being here.

Seventy musicians stared back at her, waiting, suspending judgment. One of those musicians was Jon. But she couldn't think about that now. She had to think of him as just another horn player, melding with the others.

"Thank you for coming to this hastily called rehearsal," she began. "I phoned Mr. Beech this morning, and you'll be happy to know he's feeling much better. However, his doctor still advised him to stay home today. So he told me to tell you he'll be watching us on cable, and in his words, we'd damn well and better be good."

The remark touched off a few nervous smiles, some twittery laughter.

"To which I replied, 'Mr. Beech, we aren't going to be good.'" She paused, gathering their attention. "'We're going to be *magnificent*.'" She gazed over the orchestra calmly, proudly, noticing smiles broaden. "And we *will* be.

You've prepared well. So have I. Let's put it all together, shall we?''

SIX HOURS LATER Angela's once crisp shirt stuck in damp folds to her skin, and several tendrils had escaped her neat French braid. But she herself was radiant. She'd done it! She'd led the WSO through its crisis, and knowing the straits she'd been in, the audience had given her a standing ovation.

"Great job, Ange—I mean, Miss Westgate." The young flutist, whom Angela customarily sat next to, blushed.

Still trying to cope with the audience reaction, she choked out, "Thanks, Lynn. Great job covering for me."

"Oh, Angela!" Another musician overwhelmed her with a hug, while several others patted her on the back. "Excellent," she heard. "Wonderful job." She was surprised she didn't rise right off the floor with the happiness she was feeling.

Jon finally entered the backstage area, loosening his white tie. When their eyes met, his fingers stilled, as did her heart.

Jon was the person she most wanted to see now that the concert was over. She wanted to take him by his tuxedo lapels and cry out, "See, Jon? See? This is for all the awards I never won, for all the instruments I couldn't play, for all the ordinary dullness that used to be me."

She waited expectantly, staring at him across the noisy backstage crowd, the seconds spinning out. Finally he smiled and touched his fingers to his brow in a congratulatory salute. But then someone was reaching to shake his hand, and eye contact was broken. Angela waited a little longer, but more people approached him, and soon she realized she was waiting in vain. She'd received all the praise she was going to get from Jon.

Her smile dropped. She supposed there was nothing wrong with his response, but somehow she'd expected more. An exultant hug. A stunned admission that she'd been wonderful. But that brief salute left her feeling empty.

Eventually, everyone moved to the restaurant up the street for the annual Christmas party—musicians, guests, board members and special patrons. Angela, being the party's organizer, lost the first fifteen minutes to making sure the buffet was in order.

When she finally had time to look for Jon, he was already seated at a table, the most crowded in the room. She also noticed that two of his newest friends were women of the board.

"Miss Westgate?"

Angela turned, hiding her disappointment.

"We've saved you a place." Lynn stood and pulled out a chair. "I mean, unless you have to sit with the big guns now."

Angela cast another glance toward Jon's table. Nobody looked back. They were all too engrossed in whatever he was saying.

"I can't think of anyone I'd rather sit with than you guys."

The party went quite well, much to Angela's relief. For most of the evening, however, her attention was on Jon, who seemed intent on talking to each and every person at the affair. Angela felt slighted. Not that he avoided her exactly; he did seek her out a number of times. But the sense of hollowness stayed with her. She was riding on top of the world tonight, but the person she most wanted—and needed—to share her elation with was acting as if he barely even knew her.

"He's really something, isn't he?"

Angela turned at the sound of Mrs. Fitzhugh's voice. Had she been staring? "Uh, yes."

"Such talent! Such style! He really made the concert, wouldn't you agree?"

Angela sighed, suddenly very tired. "Yes, he was excellent." And he had been. Jon's solo performance had been pure magic, and the audience had given him a standing ovation, as well.

"You did a grand job, too, dear." Mrs. Fitzhugh's twinkling eyes caught and held hers meaningfully. "A grand job," she repeated before drifting off to continue her socializing.

Angela's mouth dropped in amazement. And then she smiled, a joyous warmth spreading through her. She *had* been grand, hadn't she? Even the board now acknowledged that fact.

Inadvertently, she gazed across the room to where Jon was laughing with some of the younger musicians. Why hadn't he noticed? What did she have to do to get him to *see* her? Had nothing changed since their youth? Was he still so wound up in his own accomplishments that he couldn't make room for hers even for one night? All the talent she'd pulled out of herself, all the grit, was it still not enough? *Oh, Jon!* she cried. Was it still not enough to make him love her?

Suddenly Angela had to get out of there. Though she'd scored the victory of her career, the taste was bittersweet.

CHAPTER NINE

"WESTGATE! WHERE ARE YOU off to so fast?"

Angela turned. As hurt as she was, a flame of hope still leapt to life within her. "What do you want, Jon?"

He ambled across the parking lot, his cashmere coat hooked negligently over one shoulder. "We have an expedition coming up day after tomorrow that we've hardly talked about yet."

"Oh, that." Her hopeful expression sagged. "For the last week you've done nothing *but* talk about that expedition."

He grinned. "So, are you ready?"

Her face hardened. "In case you haven't noticed, I've had a few other things to think about lately. But don't worry, I'll be ready."

"Would you like me to help you pack?"

"Uh-uh. I can manage."

"How about shopping? I have to go for myself. Do you—"

"No!"

Jon raised his palms. "Okay, okay. We won't go shopping. You're weird, Westgate, you know that?" And before she could retort, he added, "I'll call tomorrow to run through our old checklist to make sure we have everything we need. Okay?"

Angela knotted with frustration. Jon had to be aware of what a monumental task she'd faced today, but apparently he was choosing to ignore it. It was almost as if he couldn't accept this new adult side of her and so was going to skip right over it and blithely get on with their friendship as he understood it.

But then another thought struck her. Was it possible that Jon was secretly resentful she'd been allowed the opportunity to prove herself? Was he jealous?

Well, fine. Let him act like a child. It still wouldn't change the fact that she'd been good.

"Sure. Call. Whatever you want, Jon," she tossed off while heading for her car.

JON ARRIVED at her place early Tuesday morning, the very air around him ringing with his enthusiasm.

"Oh." Angela's voice sank. "You bought new clothes."

"Mmm. None of my old things fit anymore."

"Great." She cast a disparaging look over her shabby wools, purchased eons ago at the Salvation Army store. "You look like you just stepped out of a catalog, while I look like a bag lady from outer space."

"Nobody's going to see us."

"I don't care."

"The important thing is to be warm," Jon assured her, trying to hide his amusement. "Those clothes always served you well."

He turned to the mirror, and while he made a show of adjusting his new turtleneck, she stuck her tongue out at him. Since the concert, Angela had tried to lose her irritability, but this, his showing up in color-coordinated state-of-the-art outdoor wear, was doing nothing to help.

"What flute are you bringing?" he asked. "Nothing valuable, I hope."

"No. The old one I used in high school."

He nodded. "I rented a horn. Got extra socks?"

"Yes."

"Rain gear?"

Angela huffed. "We went through all this yesterday. Yes. I've got everything."

"Okay, then. Looks like we're ready."

Angela gave her snug warm condo a baleful glance and asked herself yet again why she was going on this hike. She couldn't come up with a single reason—except that Jon wanted to go, and, like the Angela of old, she'd let him bulldoze her into accompanying him.

"I ought to have my head examined," she muttered, locking up.

They followed Route 93 north, leaving the gently rolling landscape of southern New Hampshire for a world of ever thickening hills, which in turn grew steadily into craggy snow-capped peaks.

After two and a half hours of driving, they finally reached the Randolph Valley in the Northern Peaks region of the Presidential Range. They'd decided to tackle Mount Adams again, the second-highest mountain in New England. As often as Angela had visited the area, she still felt overwhelmed by its natural beauty—the dense pine and stands of graceful birch, the rushing streams and the fields glistening with snow. And the mountains, of course, the silent, wind-blasted mountains. In winter their beauty was a ferocious sort of thing she preferred not to dwell on.

But of course she did. How could she not, knowing that scores of people had died in these mountains, people who'd lost their way, or slipped off an icy cliff, or were caught in a surprise storm? The weather observatory on Mount Washington had once clocked the wind there at 231 miles an hour. Combined with temperatures that often dropped well below zero, the area had won the distinction of having the worst weather in the world.

Jon pulled into a parking area off the state highway just after eleven, his tires carving ruts in the four inches of new snow that had fallen the previous night. Behind a haze of cloud, the sun was now a dull white glare. Angela checked the heavy sky and then her watch. In good physical shape, she could make the climb in three hours. Out of shape, it might take five or six, and with the days being at their shortest this time of year, she only hoped they didn't run out of light before reaching the shelter Jon had chosen as their destination.

"Heaven help us," she whispered, regretting not having enrolled in aerobics class this fall.

"Put your gaiters on, Angel," Jon advised, opening the car door on his side.

"I am, I am," she said, slipping on the nylon protectors that would keep snow out of her boots. Then she tugged on her wool hat and glove liners. Her hands, she noticed, were trembling. So was her stomach, and she wondered again why she was putting herself through such agony.

Jon propped her frame pack on the fender, an old habit to make the task of slipping it on easier for her. "Great day for a hike, isn't it?" he said.

"Just dandy." She didn't even try to disguise her dread as she shrugged into the straps and buckled the pack in place. "Ugh! I feel like a beast of burden."

Jon's grin grew wicked. "I'll be right back. Just have to pay our parking fee."

By the time he returned her cheeks were beginning to feel the bite of the cold.

"Jon, the thermometer on that garage there reads fifteen degrees, and we're still at the base."

He merely winked, his eyes dancing with devils.

"You're crazy, Stoddard, you know that? You're crazy, I'm crazy, and we're both going to die ... Hey, wait up."

They followed Lowe's Path across a logged area, over railroad tracks and into the rising woods. Angela remembered the trail as the easiest way to climb Mount Adams, with mostly moderate grades and inspiring views throughout. She and Jon had once hiked the trail right to the bare, jumbled rocks of the summit cone, but today they wouldn't be going quite that high.

Angela plodded on, snow-laden branches arching overhead, sometimes so thick and close she felt as if she was navigating a tunnel. The air was cold, but after a while, they had to stop to shed some of their layers. As Jon reminded her, it wouldn't do to perspire and dampen their clothing.

"How're you doing?" he asked while securing his sweater to his pack.

Angela flexed her shoulders. "I ache."

He cast her a mock-pitying frown. "Poor baby, come here." She did. "Turn." She did that, too, and with deep-kneading fingers Jon massaged the burning muscles of her shoulders. "There, that'll have to hold you for a while."

She faced him again, glaring her unhappiness with this whole undertaking. But Jon only chucked her under the chin. "Get your pack on, kid. We have miles to go before we sleep."

They trudged on, the snow getting deeper, the course rougher and more steeply pitched. Angela soon forgot the weight of her pack and simply lost herself in the rhythm of her walking, in the rhythm of her breathing. The air was blessedly still and fragrant with spruce and fir. Ahead of her, Jon whistled, his pace always intrepid. Maybe this wouldn't be so bad, after all, she thought.

A short time later, however, she developed a stitch in her side, which increased to a sharp pain. She broke out in a sweat, each step becoming an agony, and feared Jon would have to carry her back to the car. "Wait. Stop," she called out, gasping for breath.

Jon swiveled around, his expression filling with concern. "What's the matter?"

Brushing the snow off a fallen tree, Angela grunted, "I need to rest." She sank down onto the trunk and doubled over. "A cramp in my side," she explained to her snow-covered boots.

"Sorry. I was probably going too fast." Jon sat beside her and placed his arm lightly across her shoulders. "Just as well. I could use some hot chocolate right about now. How about you?"

Angela's throat tightened. She felt so inadequate, so like a failure—and so utterly frightened. What if this was appendicitis?

But of course it wasn't. By the time they finished their watery chocolate, the stitch in her side had disappeared, and she was ready to set out again.

Farther along, she interrupted Jon's singing. He'd been entertaining her with a medley that ran from a sublime "O Holy Night" to a ridiculous "Popeye the Sailor Man."

"Jon, will you tell me something?" she panted, catching up to walk by his side. "Why are we doing this?"

"Why? Aside from the fact that we promised ourselves we would a decade ago?" Jon squinted ahead, thinking. "Well ... we need this, Angel. Personally, I've been working too hard, living in cities too long. The spirit gets dull. Life becomes so cluttered we can't see what's really important. Sometimes a person just has to simplify and reduce life to bare essentials in order to sort the wheat from the chaff and rejuvenate that old weary spirit. Know what I mean?"

Angela thought she did. "Okay. That's why you're on this hike. But what's my reason?"

He laughed, his breath billowing. "I don't know. That's for you to find out, but my guess is, your reason's pretty much the same." With that, he slipped his pack to the ground so he could put on his sweater again.

They were fairly high up the mountain now, and the temperature was dropping. Angela shivered, donning her discarded clothing, too. A wind was picking up, whistling through the thinning trees with a forlornness that made her long for home. Quickly, they zipped closed their parkas, tugged down their hats, pulled their neck guards up over their noses, and continued on their way.

Angela now ached from the small of her back all the way to her neck. Her chest was heavy, her head light from breathing so deeply for so extended a time, and the cold dry air made her eyes feel gritty. But it was her legs that con-

cerned her most. They burned and quivered so badly she
wondered how much longer she could stay on her feet.

Noticing that the sky was darkening, she checked her
watch. "Oh, no! Jon, we're not making the time we used
to."

"It's the snow that's slowing us down. You're doing fine.
You'll hold up." Jon's dark eyes, all that was visible through
his face mask, crinkled with a reassuring smile.

"So, how is everything with Ivan these days? Have you
seen him lately?"

"No, and I probably won't for a very long time. Christmas break lasts five weeks. But he called."

"That so? Has he given you any trouble about your
breakup?"

Jon had asked her that once before, but she answered
anyway. "Nope. He's peeved but resigned." She knew
they'd reached a point in their journey where it was important to keep talking as a check against disorientation—a sure
sign of hypothermia.

They walked on, chatting inconsequentially for a few
more minutes, and then Jon paused again, his eyes narrowed. Angela watched him peer in one direction, then another, and finally down to the compass he held in one hand
and the map he held in the other. Suddenly her heart was
beating like a metronome gone berserk.

"What?" she asked almost voicelessly.

"Nothing."

"You're lying."

"No, I'm just making sure we keep to the trail."

Angela scanned the snow-covered landscape and thought,
What trail? They'd climbed clear to the tree line, a wild
dangerous place where humans didn't belong. Here nothing existed except snow-encrusted granite and rock rubble.
"We're lost, aren't we?"

"No, damn it. Will you stop moaning and let me think for
a minute?"

Angela reared back. Jon rarely raised his voice, which only confirmed her fear: they *were* lost.

He whipped down his face guard. "I didn't mean to snap. Sorry." As he spoke, a snowflake drifted between them. Then another. Within seconds, the world had gone white.

"Oh, no! We're going to die."

Jon gripped her arms tight. "We are not going to die."

"Why not? People die in these mountains all the time."

"Hey..." Jon finally noticed she was trembling. "You're really frightened. I didn't realize ... Oh, come here."

His jacket was as frigid as the air, but Angela didn't care. She nestled into him, needing his arms around her at this moment.

"Jon, I don't know where we are. We should've reached the hut by now, which means we must've veered off the trail. I'm sorry. I should've taken more interest...."

"Shh, shh. You're right. We did veer off the trail, but not by much. And you do know where you are." He tipped her face up to meet his confident eyes. "Grey Knob Trail is just a stone's throw away, back down in that direction." He pointed.

"It is?" Then why was his heart pounding under her hand?

"Yes. We'll be at the shelter before you know it." Jon pressed her face to his chest and turned against the wind as a particularly strong gust buffeted them. "Ready?" he asked against her wool-covered ear.

She gazed up into his dark eyes. This was the craziest, deepest trouble he'd ever led her into, and just as soon as they were home she was going to tell him so. But right now she was going to borrow all the courage and confidence she could from him. "Ready," she answered.

That "stone's throw" seemed interminable to Angela. The snow continued to fall, the darkness to deepen, and every step she took was a blind leap of faith in Jon's navigational instincts. She herself was totally disoriented.

Glimpsing the fear in her eyes, Jon finally stopped and patiently pointed out their location on the map. To her delight, she *did* know where she was. She felt better after that and even imagined a renewed vigor in her step.

By the time they reached the cabin in the designated camping area, however, darkness was fully upon them. Jon directed the beam of his flashlight on the latch, opened the door and let out a joyous whoop. "We made it!"

Stumbling in behind him, Angela wanted to cry, sure her toes were frostbitten. The air inside the wooden hut was as cold as the air outside, but at least now they were sheltered from the wind.

"Here, let me brush the snow off your clothes." Jon dropped his pack to the floor with a hard thunk. "Once we get a fire going, we don't want this stuff melting into the fabric."

A fire. Angela gazed toward the wood stove, took in the generous supply of chopped wood beside it and felt a ripple of hysterical laughter rise in her throat. "Yes. Let's get the snow off."

A lantern stood on a rough-hewn table in the center of the dark room. Jon pulled off his shells and mittens until he was down to his fingerless gloves, then pried a box of water-proof matches from his pack. Angela, stamping her feet nearby, noticed how stiff his fingers were, what difficulty he had holding a match and striking it. Finally he got one lighted and held it, shaking, to the wick. Soon the room swam with yellow light. But oh, Lord, in the illumination, how bloodless his face appeared. Angela's heart ached for him.

"What should I do?" she asked.

"Well, you could make us some hot chocolate. In the meantime, I'll try to get a fire going."

Angela was happy to do something useful. She set up her small propane burner on the table, poured bottled water into a tin pot, set it atop the ring and held her hands over the heat.

"I finally understand why cave people made such a fuss over fire," she commented, trying to contain the desperate joy she felt.

Jon laughed huskily. "This *is* rather primitive, isn't it?"

Angela watched him surreptitiously over her task. He didn't seem able to grip the kindling but had to shovel it up, instead, two-handed.

"Here, drink this." Angela handed him a tin cup and, squatting beside him in front of the stove, repressed a desire to put her arms around him and wrap him in whatever warmth she could provide.

Jon held the cup in two hands and leaned his face into the rising steam. "Thanks." As he sipped, the kindling inside the stove caught fire. Sighing in relief, Angela reached for a split log, carefully placed it atop the kindling, then picked up her own cup from the floor and took a comforting swallow.

For a long while they sat in worshipful silence, staring at the spreading flames. Finally, when heat began to radiate noticeably from the stove, Jon turned to her and smiled.

"Looks like we're going to live." He wound his arm around her neck and pulled her roughly against him. "So, where's my supper, woman?"

Angela scrabbled out of his grip, her mood lifting with his. "Woman? *Woman?* I am not amused, Jonathan."

"I can't help it. It's getting to me. You know, all this reducing life to bare essentials?"

Angela avoided his eyes, suddenly uneasy with the thought of reducing him to man, herself to woman.

Grinning, he helped her to her feet and together they emptied their bags of the dehydrated rations they'd packed. Soon they had chicken soup simmering on the ring burner and bread, wrapped in foil, warming on the stove. While that happened, they shook the cold from their sleeping bags and spread them on two of the wooden platforms built for that purpose.

"Before I get too cozy," Angela said when Jon removed his jacket, "I'm going to pay a visit to the, um, facilities."

"Take the flashlight, and don't go sight-seeing, okay?"

"You can count on that."

Angela couldn't believe how cold it was outside. And how dark! Not a single star glimmered in the inky blackness. But it was the sound of the wind that bothered her most, the low full-throated moan of it as it moved through ravines and resonated off granite walls; the wind, that up here hissed through the trees and slid the dry snow in ghostly veils upon itself with the same insidious hiss. Everything outside seemed alive with a patient malevolence, and Angela couldn't get back inside the hut fast enough.

She fell against the door, breathing hard, and feasted on the sight before her: a crackling fire, bowls of steaming soup, crude lantern light—and Jon.

"It's fierce out there." She removed her outerwear and hung it from a peg. "The hills are alive, Jon, and not with the sound of music." Though she joked, her sense of danger and isolation had deepened appreciably.

"Come eat."

"Gladly. Hey, what's that smell?" When she spotted the candle on the table, she laughed. "Bayberry? You carried a bayberry candle all the way up this mountain?"

"I thought I'd better. You reminded me often enough that you'd rather be doing something more civilized on Christmas Eve. Wait a sec." Jon bent over his pack, came up with a hand-size tape player, and within moments the cabin was filled with the sounds of Bing Crosby singing "Adeste Fideles"—wobbly sounds because the batteries were still quite cold.

"I also thought we'd top off our supper with these," he said, pulling out a small plastic bag of sugar cookies, mostly broken. "Followed by a reading of, voilà, *The Night Before Christmas*."

Angela pressed her fingers to her mouth, muffling her astonished cry. Simultaneously, her eyes stung with tears.

*Oh, Jon. How much I love you! And how thankful I am
that we're still alive and together on this godforsaken peak.*

She sat down quickly and dug into her meal, trying to hide
the emotion swelling within her.

"This soup is wonderful," she said after a few ravenous
swallows. "Did you buy something new?" She scooped up
another spoonful, lingering over its aromatic warmth, then
savoring its saltiness and rich chicken flavor. Never had
anything tasted so good or lent such comfort.

"No. What's new is we just survived one of the riskiest
climbs we ever made."

She met his eyes slowly. "Damn you. It was risky, wasn't
it?"

"And you're reaping one of the rewards—deeper appreciation of simple things." Jon smiled, his eyes burning with
pride as they traveled over her wind-reddened features.
"Thanks for being such a good sport and coming along. I
wouldn't have done it without you." His face, made achingly handsome in the warm candlelight, became serious.
"And I couldn't imagine doing this with anyone else."

Angela felt as if she were melting under his gaze. But she
still managed to dig up one more scowl. "Don't thank me
yet. This is the stupidest thing I've ever done, and I plan to
be mad at you for a good long time."

Jon reached across the table and squeezed her hand. "I'm
so glad you're having fun."

She glowered back at him, but all the while struggling
with a smile. The heat from the stove was easing the tightness in her shoulders, the scent of bayberry filled her nos-
trils, and a profound sense of well-being suffused her soul.

She pushed aside her empty bowl and murmured hesitantly, "This doesn't make sense, but I feel really good right
now. Heady. As if I could do almost anything."

Jon nodded in understanding.

"What's even crazier, I feel safe here."

Jon reached into her with his gaze. "You are safe. We're
well equipped, we're experienced, and I let several people

know our trail route. I'd never lead you into anything we couldn't handle. You know that, don't you?"

She swallowed. Yes, she supposed she did.

"So, what would you like to do with the rest of the evening? I brought a deck of cards...."

"I... brought something, too." She hesitated a moment, then brushed aside her reservations and presented him with a foil-wrapped box.

He blinked. "A present?"

She nodded. "Now, don't start feeling guilty or anything. It isn't much."

"Shall I open it now, or do I have to wait until morning?"

"Now's fine." In mounting anticipation she watched him peel back the paper.

"What the...!" The next moment he was howling with laughter. "Where did you ever find these?" he asked, holding up a pair of berry red boxer shorts printed all over with yellow French horns.

Angela beamed, delighted by his reaction. They'd started giving each other joke gifts when they were in elementary school, and the tradition had continued until they'd parted. She wasn't sure he'd remember.

When he dug into his bag and came up with a gift for her, her heart contracted. "What's this?"

"A little something to even the score."

Eagerly, she unwrapped the box and removed the top. A smile worked into her features and her shoulders began to shake. "Do you really expect me to wear these?"

"Absolutely."

Still chuckling, she lifted out a pair of sunglasses, each lens stamped with a bar of music. She put them on and, vision obscured, groped for her pack again.

The box she handed Jon this time contained what looked like an old-fashioned snow dome, but inside was a troll-like figure sitting at a piano. When the dome was shaken, tiny black notes swirled about, instead of snow.

This gift was followed by a pair of sterling silver earrings for her in the shape of treble clefs, and that was followed by a French-horn tie tack for him, followed by a T-shirt for her that read I Know the Score.

Angela smiled warmly at the array of presents heaped on the table between them, amazed that she had been on his mind as much as he'd been on hers during this shopping season. But her pack still wasn't empty. Biting her lip, she lifted out her last present.

Jon unwrapped it carefully, sensing it was special. When he unfolded the embroidered linen, his expression dropped. "Oh, Angel. Did you do this?"

Holding her breath, she nodded while he read the cross-stitch sampler. God Danced the Day You Were Born, it said.

"That's the nicest thing anyone has ever said to me." He swallowed, his eyes suddenly suspiciously bright. "But it must've taken you days...."

She shrugged his comment off even though he was right. "I'll have it framed for you, of course. It was just easier to pack like that."

"Thank you." Jon reached across the table, squeezed her hand and smiled. Then, without preamble he presented her with a final gift, too.

Angela didn't expect anything from him, not even the joke gifts. Now, folding back the tissue paper from this last present, she fought an urge to cry.

On a rosewood-and-mirror base posed an Austrian crystal angel playing a flute, its exquisitely cut facets afire in the candlelight. Angela was utterly speechless.

"It's a music box," Jon informed her softly. "Wind it up." She did, and a moment later the cabin chimed with the delicate sounds of Beethoven's "Ode to Joy," one of her favorite pieces of music.

"Well..." she said, her throat tightening. "Well..." she repeated helplessly, her eyes filling with tears.

Without speaking, they watched the angel revolve until the melody played out.

"Thank you, Jon," she finally managed to say. "I'll treasure it forever."

They spent the rest of the evening alternately admiring their gifts, nibbling sugar cookies and listening to the Bing Crosby tape. They even fit in a game of gin rummy. Finally, however, Jon got up to rebuild the fire, a prelude to turning in for the night.

Unexpectedly, Angela felt an awkwardness that had been missing most of the evening. She was still wearing three layers of clothing and knew that to sleep comfortably and avoid the danger of perspiring, she ought to be down to one—her underwear. But how to undress in front of Jon without turning ten shades of red?

She removed her boots and quietly placed them by the stove. Then she climbed onto the wooden platform and into her bag, fully clothed. There, she struggled with her sweater and woolen shirt, then grappled with her pants, feeling distinctly like a butterfly fighting its way out of a cocoon.

Meanwhile, having finished stoking the fire, Jon was standing by, watching. "Sweetheart, there's an easier way to do that."

She glared, quite aware that he was laughing. "I'm done." She fell back, panting, and stared up at the dark beamed ceiling, her sleeping bag tucked up to her chin.

When Jon pried off his boots, she turned her face to the wall. A moment later the cabin was filled with the rustling sounds of him undressing. Only after he'd settled did she dare look back. Their beds were at right angles, his feet to hers, so that their eyes met easily. She watched him tuck a shirt under his head, watched the light from the bayberry candle streaking across his chiseled face and swallowed over a dryness that wouldn't abate.

"Are you warm enough?" he asked.

"Yes."

He continued to watch her, his dark eyes gleaming like onyx stars. "Know something, Angel?"

"What?"

"This is the best Christmas ever."

She smiled, warmth flooding through her. "It isn't bad."

"Then you aren't mad at me anymore?"

"About what?"

Jon braced himself up on one elbow, a frown working across his brow. "Frankly, I don't know. Did I do something Sunday to upset you?"

A small current of tension zinged through Angela's body. "Uh, no," she said without conviction.

"Are you sure?"

She hesitated. "Well..." Then, riding a wave of remembered pain, she blurted, "Damn it, Jon! I was good. Why couldn't you be happy for me?"

He lay quiet. "You think I wasn't happy for you?"

She let silence answer for her.

Abruptly, Jon sat up and swung his legs over the side of the platform. Angela had seen him in thermals before, but not for a very long time. Good Lord, even in those the man was a dream.

"How could you think I'd be anything but happy? You were wonderful." He pushed himself off the platform and paced the floor, still looking very confused.

Angela stared at the ceiling over her bed, perplexed. "You didn't say much to me. You spent the evening schmoozing with the board ladies and anyone else you could buttonhole. What were you doing, Jon?"

His eyes narrowed. "What do you think I was doing?"

She shrugged, looked away, then mumbled, "Did you think I'd gained too much of an advantage that day in the race for Mr. Beech's job?"

Jon's face fell. A moment later he crossed the room and sat on the edge of her platform. She felt his closeness over every trembling inch of her body, yet willed herself to appear indifferent.

"That was the furthest thing from my mind. If I spent too much time talking to other people, I'm sorry, but I wasn't undercutting you. I was simply enjoying myself. It felt good talking to people from Winston, very good. We talked about real estate taxes, the high school hockey team, all sorts of things. What we *didn't* talk about was the WSO directorship or you." He reached over and framed her face with his hands, making her look at him. "No matter what you think, Angel, I'm not the enemy."

Her throat was so parched she couldn't swallow. "I'm sorry, Jon." She shook her head. "It's just..." Just what? she wondered. That he'd walked away from her once and she'd found it hard to trust him since?

Jon brushed the hair from her forehead, his hand tracing a path down the side of her cheek. "I don't know if this helps, but I wanted to be with you more. I just didn't know if you wanted to be with me. The day before you were so insistent we stay apart."

"That was while I was preparing."

"Well, I wasn't sure. And then there was the small matter of your looking so good. I thought if we were together too much, I'd have trouble keeping my hands off you."

Angela's cheeks turned to flame. "Knock it off, Jon."

"Knock what off? You looked great. Good enough to set atop a Christmas tree." His roguish smile sent tremors quaking through her.

She managed to cast him a wry glance. "An angel in a tux?"

"Depends on whose fantasy it is." He was leaning over her now, a hand planted on either side of her. Angela swallowed convulsively.

"Jon, I think you ought to get over to your own bed."

"I will, but in a while. I'm really in the mood to talk. Move over, will you?" Before she could protest, Jon slid his hands under her and lifted, sleeping bag and all, then settled her nearer the wall.

"What are you doing?" Her heart pounded.

"Shh." He stretched out on the platform beside her, his arm pillowing his cheek. Behind him, the cabin was lit only by the wavering bayberry candle. Angela, studying Jon's face, seeing it made achingly attractive by the mysterious backlighting, became frightened by the closeness.

"I know you feel uncomfortable talking about what happened between us nine years ago, Angel." Jon drew a line down her cheek with the back of his fingers, causing her breath to stop in her throat. "But I've got to return to that incident just one more time. For years I've been bothered by the thought that you misconstrued my reasons for making love."

Angela eased onto her back, away from his hot earnest gaze. A heaviness returned to her heart. What was to misconstrue? His behavior after that trip had explained everything.

Jon cupped her hot cheek and turned her to face him. "Making love to you wasn't the simple physical encounter you seem to think it was." His thumb traced the curve of her lips with drugging slowness. Angela wondered how she could feel so languid while her heart was racing away. "It was much more. If you remember, we'd been talking about leaving Winston and meeting new people...."

Angela wet her parched lips. "Yes. I remember."

"Hmm. But what you don't know is how upset I was by your going away. You were special, my forever friend, my Angel...." He breathed her name with the same reverent passion she remembered from that day nine years ago. She closed her eyes, melting under the heat of his dark gaze.

"And the idea of sharing you and ultimately perhaps of losing you drove me crazy, especially when we started talking about your... well, you know, your having sexual relations. Suddenly I wanted to tuck you into my pocket, take you wherever I was going and shield you from all the insensitive jerks of this world. I wanted to *keep* you, Angel, even though I knew we both had to part."

Angela couldn't believe what she was hearing. If time could take on color, this moment would be all spangly silver, and at the center of that moment would be Jon.

"Why... why are you telling me this?"

"Well, initially I wanted to explain what I was feeling when we made love nine years ago. I thought you might feel better if you knew I wasn't just running on rampant teenage hormones."

This made her smile.

"But somewhere along the way, I began to realize that this conversation has more to do with wanting you right now. All the reasons I'm giving you are just words, air spun into rationalizations to make sense of the simple fact that I want you."

Angela wasn't sure if she was about to laugh or weep. She suspected there was reason to do both.

"Angel, I'm not going to tell you that you were the only reason I returned to New England. I was tired of traveling and missed home.

"And you had Cynthia."

His sardonic laugh left no doubt how much influence Cynthia had exerted on his decision to return. "But I will say this. I was curious about you, curious about this feeling I'd been living with that something had been left undone. There was an incompleteness to our relationship, a disturbing lack of closure."

"Closure? You need closure?" Dismay pressed down on her.

Jon lifted himself up over her. "What I need, my Angel, is to find out why I never stopped thinking about you or why nothing in my experience has ever come close to that one night of heaven we shared on this mountain nine years ago."

"Jon, no . . ." She tried to lift a staying hand, but his lips were already touching hers. This couldn't be happening, she thought, even as her body curled helplessly into the heat of his. She'd been devastated by his desertion of her nine years ago. What would it do to her now? And he *would* leave her, just as soon as he'd satisfied his curiosity and acquired his sense of closure.

"Jon, please, we promised we wouldn't do this. We agreed our friendship was worth too much to risk."

His lips, warm and parted, brushed over hers and down the soft underside of her chin. Angela's senses reeled under the tender assault.

"I've heard all your reasons, and when I think about them rationally, sure, I agree. But right now, sweetheart, my reasoning powers aren't working too well. Right now I'm all intuition and nerve endings." His intoxicating gaze seemed to be drawing her into him. "Just for once, join me, Angel. Don't think. Just for this night, stop analyzing, stop trying to control things, and let your feelings go."

Angela felt a quake deep inside her, like a bastion weakening. She gazed into Jon's midnight eyes, eyes she'd known all her life. He was such an important part of her. Opposites, yes, but fitting so well that together they made a complete circle—halves of a whole who needed the other for balance. A smile curved her lips as the words "yin" and "yang" passed through her mind.

"What are you smiling about?" Jon tilted his head.

I love you, she thought with her heart. *I love you so very, very much.*

What she whispered aloud was, "Come here." Lifting her arms, Angela felt the last of her defenses tumble.

For a moment, she thought he'd changed his mind. He pulled back, his whole body stilled. "Yes?" he whispered.

"Yes. Come here."

His eyes darkened as he moved closer, and when he pressed his lips to hers, they positively smoldered.

He tasted sweeter than her wildest fantasies. She touched his face, his hair, the corded muscles of his neck; she pressed her hands along his neck and over his chest, desperate to know that he was real and really with her.

Somewhere on the edge of her consciousness, a zipper whispered open—a long, slow coming-apart sound—and then Jon was with her without the barrier of the sleeping bag. Her body ran molten from the moment they touched.

What was happening was crazy, she thought through the thickening fogs of passion. It was bound to lead to heartache, was bound to ruin their friendship. They'd be left with nothing. And then he'd leave....

No, don't think, Angela. Just for tonight, let yourself go....

And she did.

CHAPTER TEN

ANGELA AND JON made love in a white heat, a blinding whirlwind that left her lying in his arms in a floaty semiconscious rapture. Outside, the wind still hissed through the trees, and the inky night, one of the longest of the year, pressed down on the vast primeval wilderness of ice and granite. But inside the hut, the world had once again become an Eden. Angela snuggled against Jon's side, feeling warm, safe and at perfect peace.

They awoke simultaneously to the tiny beeping sound of Jon's wristwatch alarm. The cabin was dark and cold. They groaned and, hugging each other, huddled deeper into the warmth of the down-filled bag.

"Do we really have to get up?" Angela murmured groggily against his smooth shoulder.

He shifted, wrapping her under him. "We don't have to do anything we don't want to." In the dark he kissed her forehead, her cheek, her ear.

"Are you perchance looking for my lips?"

She felt him smile. "I know where they are. After last night, there isn't an inch of you I don't know how to find. Ha! You're blushing. Good. Keep it up. It's mighty cold outside this bag."

In an abrupt move, he threw the covering off them. Angela shrieked, but when she reached to pull it back up, he swung her off the platform and set her on the ice-cold floor.

She was still wearing her wool socks, but she felt the chill nonetheless. "You're a sadist. I hate you," she gasped, dancing about and groping for clothing.

Jon laughed, lit the lantern, and with a casual disregard for his nudity, caught her in his arms and kissed her. Helpless against him, Angela whimpered, and the kiss that had started out as playful soon became a long intimate exploration.

Jon shuddered as he finally set her away from him. "Aw, no. If we start that again, we'll never get out of here." He took a deep breath, then laughed. "You're thinking the same thing I'm thinking. No, Angel." He patted her backside. "Get dressed, and while you're at it, try to keep jumping around and get the blood flowing."

Jump around? Angela grinned. This morning she felt sure she could fly.

They left the hut in the predawn gray, dressed as if for an Arctic expedition, each carrying an instrument case. Angela walked along in relative comfort, despite the fact that the thermometer outside the hut read only six above. The air was blessedly calm and dry, and overhead the morning star burned bigger and brighter than she'd ever seen it; her special Christmas star, she decided.

They climbed a short distance above the tree line. "How's this?" Jon asked.

From the open ledge facing southeast, Angela gazed out over countless miles of peaks and valleys, feeling as if she was standing at the heart of creation. "This is fine."

"Glad you approve." Small lines fanned out from the corners of his eyes, and her heart flooded with warmth, remembering again the closeness they'd shared through the night.

"Would you like to sit?" Jon laid his horn case on a flat granite slab. "It shouldn't be more than a few minutes."

They brushed away the snow and sat, eyes directed toward the horizon. Time ticked on, but the sky looked as dark as ever.

"Such a long night. Is the sun never going to rise?"

Jon stretched out his legs, arms folded calmly over his parka. "Patience, sweetheart. The sun always rises. Hey, that sounds like a good title for a novel."

The morning stillness was silvered with Angela's soft laughter.

They fell into companionable silence again, watching the horizon, waiting the long winter's wait for the sun. After what seemed an age, Jon looked at her and droned, "I know, I know, this is crazy."

She shook her head solemnly. "Don't think it even for a second."

Gradually the sky took on an orange-pink wash. She glanced at Jon, a question in her eyes, but he still shook his head.

She sat closer, beginning to feel the cold, and continued to watch the panorama before her. She waited while the sky washed to peach and the morning star gradually disappeared. When the horizon went to white, Jon finally pulled off his mask and opened his horn case.

"Okay, I figure we have about five minutes before condensation shuts down this gig," he said.

Angela felt her pulse quicken. "Then let's do it in style."

She raised the cold flute to her lips, and just as they had agreed when they were dreamy-eyed teenagers, they began to play "What Child Is This?" And as they played, the sun rose over the far horizon, bleaching out the snowy peaks and flashing off the rich brass bell of Jon's horn.

Vaguely Angela wondered if anyone heard them. A scientist perhaps over at the weather station on Mount Washington. Or a farmer deep in some sleepy valley rising to milk his cows. She wondered what miracle they thought they were waking to.

But she and Jon hadn't come here to play for anyone else, and if no one heard, which was probably the case, that was all right, too. They'd come here simply for the experience.

Something about the moment reminded her of a print Jon used to have in his room when he was young, Michelangelo's *Creation of Man*. But in his inimitable way, Jon had tinkered with the masterpiece. Right over the almost-touching fingers of God and man, he'd drawn a quarter note. She'd never asked him to explain, but now she thought she understood what he'd meant.

She put her flute down before the song ended, unable to continue for the tightness in her throat, leaving Jon to finish alone. And as he played, tears slid down Angela's cheeks. Whatever music was capable of doing, Jon's music did it. He touched the soul and lifted it to touch the sublime.

Jon finished the song and lowered the horn to his knee. Angela wiped her eyes and watched the sun pour its cold wintry light over his solemn face. His eyes were hard and fixed, his chin jutting, sure signs that he was shoring himself up against a tide of emotion. She had so much to say— how the experience had surpassed her wildest expectations, how thankful she was that he'd given her this moment—but knew she didn't have to, for he understood. He took her hand and together they sat in silence for a few minutes more, watching the sky fill with sunlight.

Finally they got to their feet.

"Merry Christmas, my Christmas Angel," he said, framing her face with his hands.

"Merry Christmas, Jon." Her smiling lips trembled, and when he kissed them, they trembled even more. She thought she'd never been so happy.

He sighed contentedly and kissed her forehead. "Let's go have some breakfast."

ANGELA LEFT THE HUT reluctantly. If time could be measured by the depth of emotion experienced within each minute, then she and Jon had spent a lifetime here. But he had a Florida-bound plane to catch, and she had a long drive to her sister's. So they hiked back down the mountain, a journey that went surprisingly fast, and returned to her condominium in Winston.

Yet, when it came time to part, Jon couldn't seem to let her go. Standing at the door, he held her in his arms and continued to kiss her passionately, repeatedly, despite her occasional reminders of the time.

Finally he stepped back. "Okay, you're right. I'll miss my plane if I don't get moving." He took a deep breath and, tearing his gaze away from her flushed face, hurried out the door.

But a moment later he was back and kissing her so thoroughly her knees turned to water. When he eventually lifted his head, he was grinning in pure male satisfaction. "Hold that thought till I get back," he said. As he jogged down the walk, Angela fell against the doorframe, laughing in something close to rapture.

Two days later, she was racing the vacuum cleaner around her living room when the doorbell rang. Jon was due back from Florida, but not for another hour at least. She looked out the window, then threw open the door.

"Mr. Beech!" She cast aside propriety and gave him an exuberant hug. "Come in. How are you feeling?"

"Much better. How was your Christmas?"

She smiled beatifically. "Transcendent."

His expression made her laugh. "Transcendent. Well, you can't do better than that."

"Can I get you something to drink?"

"No, thank you. Please, could we just sit a moment and talk?"

"Sure. What is it? You look... This is something important, isn't it?" The next second, it hit her. She'd been so wrapped up in her happiness she'd actually forgotten.

"The board has made a decision regarding my replacement."

She drew a breath. "And?"

"And I felt I ought to come over and deliver the news in person. Angela, I'm so sorry."

She closed her eyes, feeling weak and dizzy. "I...I didn't get it?"

"No, I'm afraid not."

"Then, if I didn't, w-who did?"

Mr. Beech reached for her hands and held them tight. "Jonathan Stoddard."

CHAPTER ELEVEN

"ARE YOU ALL RIGHT?" Mr. Beech peered at her with concern. "Can I get you some water?"

Angela's voice, when she finally answered, was remarkably calm. "Thank you, no. I'm fine. I'm sure Jon will be wonderful. He always is."

The old conductor eyed her more sharply, and though it would have been bad form for him to admit she would've been better, the thought passed between them nonetheless. "I'm so sorry, Angela. I tried."

His sympathy was almost her undoing. Her throat closed and her eyes stung. "I understand, Mr. Beech, and I appreciate everything you've done."

He hesitated. "I haven't talked to Jonathan myself yet. Mrs. Conroy was in charge of delivering the news to him. But when I do, I intend to recommend he keep you on as directorial assistant, if that's all right with you."

Assistant to Jon? Second best again? "I'm not sure what I want right now, Mr. Beech."

"Of course. You'll need time for the news to settle."

"Could you tell me one thing? What is it about Jon that swayed the board? What does he have that I don't?"

"I think the word was 'panache.'" Mr. Beech rolled his eyes. "I don't mean to diminish his talent. It's immense, and he probably will be wonderful once he grows into the position. But what struck the board most was Jon, the personality. They felt that here was someone who would draw a crowd, attract new patrons and, in short, keep the WSO solvent."

Panache! After Mr. Beech left, Angela slumped to the half-vacuumed rug in front of her tree and in a daze stared at the ornaments. How did you fight something as indefinable as panache? Suddenly the shiny decorations swam out of focus as the realization sank in: she'd lost the WSO directorship. Good Lord, she'd lost! What was she to do now? There was no place else she wanted to be, nothing else she aspired to. She buried her face in her hands and, refusing to cry, merely shook for a few unsteady seconds.

All along she'd feared not getting the position, yet secretly, deep down, she'd believed she would. Some steady little flame of hope had always burned. But apparently she was a fool. Jon had kept his application in, and when Jon was in a race, no one else stood a chance. "Damn him!" she cried.

On a sobering wave of guilt, Angela knew she was being unreasonable. It wasn't Jon's fault. After all, he had offered to withdraw from the contest and she had told him to stay.

But even as she thought this, the pain of her disappointment welled up inside her, drowning her objectivity, and the next moment she ached to lash out at the world once again.

"Damn him!" she cried again. He could have chosen to withdraw. As her friend, he *should* have chosen to withdraw. But he hadn't. Why had she let herself think he'd be so gallant? Had she begun to believe him when he said he didn't want the job?

She should've paid stricter attention to what she *knew* about Jon rather than what she *felt*. He loved facing new challenges, loved taking center stage, and if that meant riding roughshod over a friend, well, so be it. Friend, move aside.

Damn, damn, damn! He'd been a contender all along, even while wooing her friendship and trust and ultimately her love. He didn't care one bit about her goals or feelings. She felt used and lied to, her friendship betrayed, a victim once again of Jon's ambition and arrogance.

Angela closed her eyes and moaned. She didn't like feeling this resentment, this rage, and part of her knew she was reacting irrationally. Good heavens, she loved the man. But she couldn't help herself.

The doorbell rang and her heart leapt. This time it had to be Jon. She considered swallowing her pain and congratulating him as warmly as she knew how. That would be the adult thing to do. But almost instantly she knew she'd never be able to pull off the act.

Deciding to face the problem head on, she swung open the door. But she wasn't ready for the emotional punch that came with just seeing Jon again.

He strode in and, before she could say a word, pulled her to him, one strong arm encircling her waist, his other hand burrowed into her hair. Then he was kissing her as if he'd missed her as much as she'd missed him these past two days.

Oh, Jon, don't do this, she thought. But as his soft warm lips moved over hers, plying their usual magic, as memories of their Christmas Eve swirled through her mind, she couldn't resist kissing him back.

But no, this couldn't happen. Gathering up her willpower, she pushed him away. "Stop."

He seemed stunned, then hurt. "Angel, what's the matter?"

"What's the matter? How can you show up here pretending nothing's happened?"

"Pardon me?"

She smiled icily. "The WSO directorship?"

"What about it?"

Angela fell quiet for a long embarrassing moment. "D-didn't you talk to Mrs. Conroy?"

"Uh-uh. I drove here straight from the airport." His eyes narrowed, and then he said, "Oh, hell."

Realizing what she'd just done, Angela spun away. "I'm sorry. It isn't my place to give you this news."

He gripped her shoulder and turned her to face him. "Angel, I'm really sorry."

She crossed her arms stiffly. "I'm sick to death of that word 'sorry.' You don't mean it, never have, and I don't want to hear it anymore."

Jon sighed heavily. "This isn't the way things were supposed to work out."

She laughed, trying to pretend her heart wasn't breaking. "Of course not. You didn't count on my being upset, did you? Simpleminded little Angel was supposed to be overjoyed for you. She was supposed to greet you with hugs, hallelujahs and a brass band, wasn't she?"

Jon hooked his hands on his hips and stared at her with intense searching eyes. "What's this all about?"

"What it's about, Mr. Stoddard, is the fact that you've run roughshod over me once again."

His color deepened. "But I told you weeks ago that I didn't want the position."

"Words are cheap, Jon. If you really didn't want the position, you could've withdrawn your application."

"You told me not to, damn it! You said you'd never speak to me again if I did."

Even while she understood his exasperation, her pain and anger drove her on with their own peculiar logic. "So? Did you have to listen? Couldn't you see how much the job meant to me?"

Jon thrust his fingers through his hair in frustration. "The reason I kept my application in was I never for a minute doubted you were better qualified and would get the position. I'll admit I did want it at the very beginning, but the night I slept over I saw your résumé. I saw the score you were preparing, and I realized you were far and away my superior. *You're* the one with the inferiority complex, Angel. I have no idea why, but *you* created it, *you* perpetuate it. I kept my application in for your sake. I wanted you to feel better about yourself when you were awarded the position. I wanted you to know you'd beat everybody, fair and square, including me. I was so sure you'd get it."

Angela's throat grew thick with pain. "Well, I didn't. Thank you for being so considerate!"

Jon gripped her upper arms. "Look, I don't want the damn job. I have every intention of refusing it."

"It doesn't matter anymore. Don't you see?" Her voice cracked. "You've already proved your point."

"Which is?"

"That you're better than me at everything."

"Don't be ridiculous. The only thing that's happened is a handful of women made a grossly stupid decision. I plan to turn down their offer, so the job's yours."

"As I said, it doesn't matter. There's no joy in being the orchestra's consolation prize, Jon. You've spoiled it for me. You've spoiled everything."

He let her go with a harsh little shove. "Oh, grow up!" He walked away, his hand clasped to the nape of his neck.

"Me, grow up? Now, there's a laugh."

He swiveled around, and suddenly Angela was struck by the depth of hurt in his eyes. "I've had enough of this. I'm cutting out."

Her head jerked back. "What do you mean?"

"Just what I said. I told you my reasons for applying for the job and keeping my application in, but apparently you just don't want to believe me. For some reason, you insist on believing the worst. Well, I've got a flash for you. Friends don't do that." He zipped up his jacket. "There used to be a time when trust was the basis of our friendship. I've tried to get it back, but I guess it's just not there anymore."

He smiled ruefully. "You said we'd changed. I didn't want to believe it, but now I see you were right." He paused a moment, his eyes pained as he took one last look at her. Then, "Goodbye, Angela." The next moment he was gone.

HE'D BE BACK, Angela told herself, lying awake that night. The WSO would be reconvening in two weeks, and he'd be there, taking the podium and loving every minute of it, because that's just the way Jon was. In spite of what he'd told her, she had no doubt that leading the WSO was exactly what he wanted. He'd banked on it, in fact, going so far as to actually buy a house here in Winston.

But one thing was certain: when the WSO did reconvene, Angela Westgate would not be there. How could she continue to sit in the trenches when she'd been so close to being on the podium? It would hurt too much. But what would hurt even more was having to face Jon every Wednesday night, the very nature of the meeting a reaffirmation that she'd lost to him.

Before she got up the courage to hand in a formal resignation, however, Mr. Beech called to ask if she would help him straighten the music library at the theater. She said yes, met him at the theater and, after twenty minutes of sorting through dusty files, finally broached the subject.

Mr. Beech dropped a sheaf of yellowed *1812 Overtures* into a drawer and turned, stunned. "You're not serious, are you?"

"Absolutely." She lifted another stack of jumbled files off a shelf and set them on a table.

"But, my dear, you can't quit the orchestra."

"I'm sorry, but I have to."

He frowned. "Have I missed something? Has someone declared this National Resignation Week without telling me?"

Apprehension trickled down her back. "Why?"

"Well, just yesterday Jonathan Stoddard called the board together and handed in his resignation, too."

Angela gulped. "Jon did what?"

"That's right. We met right here, in fact."

"Jon resigned his brand-new position?"

"Well, since he'd never actually accepted it, I suppose what he was doing was refusing it. Throwing it in the board's collective face, actually. Gave them a sound thrashing, too, I might add."

Her eyes widened. "For what?"

"For not choosing the right candidate for the job. I'm so glad I showed up. It was priceless." Mr. Beech laughed one of his rare raspy laughs. "That's why you can't quit. Mrs. Conroy will be calling you any time now."

Angela felt for the chair she knew was behind her. "To offer *me* the position?"

"Of course, as she should've done in the first place."

Angela's jaw hardened. "Well . . . I won't take it."

"Why not?" When she didn't answer, he asked, "Pride? Is that it, Angela?"

She rose and scrambled up the stool, away from his disconcerting gaze. "It's . . . complicated, but okay, you could call it pride."

"And you think by refusing the board's offer, you'll be hurting them? Oh, Angela, don't you realize the only person you'll be hurting is yourself?"

"Me?" She handed him a stack of old concert programs.

"Yes, you. There's an expression for what you're doing. It's cutting off your nose to spite your face."

"Well, for heaven's sake, Mr. Beech, what would you do in my situation?" She came down off the stool.

"No question about it. I'd see the board members for the fools they are, accept the position and enjoy it to the fullest. I wouldn't measure my worth by their standards, and I certainly wouldn't sit home sulking like a child."

This last remark brought a sting to her eyes. He was the second person to comment on her lack of maturity in almost as many days. "I'm sorry you feel that way." Her voice wobbled.

"Angela, buck up. This isn't like you, and quite frankly, I don't understand your behavior. Is something going on that I don't know about?"

"It's . . . personal. Between me and Jon."

"Ah. I see."

Angela frowned, wondering precisely what it was he saw. "It's a long-standing rivalry," she explained.

"Really? Hmm. That's strange."

"What is?"

"Well, if Jonathan is what you call a rival, I wish I had a few like him. If I did, I'd never want for a friend."

She blinked rapidly. "As I said, it's complicated."

Mr. Beech smiled. "Yes. Love usually is."

Dumbfounded, Angela stared at the old man as he hobbled off to a hot plate where earlier he'd prepared a pot of tea. "It doesn't have anything to do with love, Mr. Beech. What it's about is Jon's big fat ego."

"Oh. And you don't have an ego problem yourself?"

Under his sharp eye, Angela's color climbed.

"Angela, my dear, I think I need to tell you something about Jonathan." He handed her a cup of tea. "He requested I keep it a secret, but..." He shrugged. "The first time Jonathan and I talked was late August. He called."

"About the directorship?"

"No. He was looking for you."

"M-me?"

"That's right. He wanted to know if you were a member of the WSO. He said you were an old friend he was trying to locate. It was only after I assured him you were indeed a member that he applied for my job. Call me romantic, Angela, but I'd say the guy did so just to have an excuse to become part of your life again."

The teacup rattled as she set it in its saucer. "That's ridiculous!"

"Is it?"

"Then, you mean...? Oh, hell! What've I done?"

"Yes. What have you done, Angela?"

"Cut off my nose to spite my face?"

"Hmm. I thought you were looking a little peaked today."

"Mr. Beech, do you mind if we continue this later?"

"Not at all."

"Thanks." She was already pulling on her coat.

Angela drove aimlessly for more than an hour, trying to sort her muddled thoughts. For the most part, they remained muddled. But as the miles accumulated on her odometer, one realization did emerge: Jon and Mr. Beech were right; she *was* acting childishly. She'd been hurt and had gone off to sulk. And why? Because she'd felt unloved. But by whom? Who did she think didn't love her? The board?

As always the answer was Jon. She'd wanted to excel at something so he could admire her. But she'd failed. It was nine years ago all over again, and he was about to discover she wasn't as interesting as he thought. She was just ordinary, mediocre Angela with nothing to hold him here.

She suddenly felt an overwhelming need to apologize. What a terrible load of guilt she'd dumped on him, accusing him of robbing her of her joy. Spotting a phone booth, she pulled off the road.

The phone rang four times before he picked it up.

"Hello?"

Angela frowned. "Jon?"

"No. This is Anthony. Jon is out at the moment."

"Anthony?"

"Yes, the person Jon sublet the apartment from. I just returned from England."

"Oh. Oh, of course."

"Jon will be gone most of the day. He's out apartment hunting."

"Apartment hunting? Where?"

"Let's see. Today he's doing Back Bay, I believe."

"That's in Boston?"

"Yes. Would you like him to call you when he gets in?"

"No. That's all right. I'll call again later. Thank you."

Quickly, before he could ask her name, Angela hung up.

Apartment hunting? In Boston? She walked back to her car in a daze. Why would Jon be doing that when he was on the verge of buying the Thurgood house?

Suddenly her stomach bottomed out. She raced back to town, flew up the hill to Elm Street and, filled with foreboding, pulled to the curb in front of the gracious English Tudor she'd spun so many dreams about of late.

"Oh, no!" she whispered, her worst fear confirmed. The Sale Pending banner had been removed, so that the sign on the lawn again read For Sale. When Jon said he was cutting out, he really meant it.

But could she blame him? What had she ever done to make him want to stay? She'd fought their friendship every step of the way, arguing and complaining throughout, even on their dream-come-true Christmas hike. She'd also made it impossible for him to accept the WSO conductor's job, whether he'd wanted it or not. She still wasn't certain of his true feelings in that regard, but she did know he'd wanted to come back to Winston. And how better than by becoming an integral part of a community institution?

Odd, she hadn't realized it before, but everything in Jon's behavior pointed to the fact that he'd matured and was here to settle. He'd told her how tired he was of traveling, how much he'd missed New England and longed for a place to call his own. But she hadn't taken him seriously.

And now he'd given up. She gazed at the house, shimmering in her tears. She'd pushed him once too often.

Angela tried to fill the next few days with chores. She went grocery shopping, cleaned the house and washed her sweaters. But all the while she continued to think about Jon and mourn his absence.

When Mrs. Conroy finally called and offered her the conductorship, Angela surprised even herself. "Could you give me a couple of days to think about it?" she replied.

Suddenly being conductor of the Winston Symphony didn't seem all that important anymore. She'd come to realize her life wouldn't end if she turned down the position. She had her teaching jobs, and what was to stop her from applying to some other orchestra? True, she loved working with the members of the WSO, but perhaps she'd placed a little too much value on them, making them a substitute for family after her mother died.

In the meantime, she had to do something about Jon. She could live without the WSO, but she couldn't live with knowing she'd hurt Jon and disrupted his life. If he wanted to return to Winston, it was high time she did something to help.

It was New Year's Eve when Angela made up her mind to drive down to Cambridge and apologize to Jon in person. He might not accept her apology, but she had to offer one, anyway. That was the least a friend could do.

She remembered his mentioning that he would be playing with his jazz group that night, which suited her just fine. That was probably the best way to approach him, when he was relaxed and in good spirits.

She applied her makeup with care, then slipped into a sheath of a sapphire color that accentuated her eyes. She brushed her hair until it crackled and, as a concession to the festive night, caught it up in two rhinestone combs. A touch of subtle cologne behind her ears, a change into higher heels, and she was ready. Then, knees knocking, she headed for the door.

Angela wasn't aware that traffic would be so heavy and only belatedly remembered that Boston celebrated First Night in such lavish fashion. It was late when she finally walked into the club. The place was crowded, all the tables taken, and for a moment she felt self-conscious, standing alone at the bar. Everyone else was with somebody on this special night. But then a waiter led her to a small table that had just been set up to one side. As she sat he placed a silver party hat and a noisemaker before her and smiled diffidently.

She ordered a schnapps to chase away the chill of the night, then sought out Jon on the stage. As always, her heart soared just at the sight of him.

The group finished the number they were playing and announced a break. Angela wrung her hands as Jon walked off the stage. Abruptly she stood, and even though she didn't say a word, he turned in her direction. When he recognized her, his head jerked back.

Please don't turn away, she prayed with all her heart. *Please, hear me out.*

Slowly, he approached her table, everything about his demeanor held in check. "Westgate! Well, well." His mouth, usually so sensual and relaxed, looked hard, his eyes cold as steel.

"H-hello, Jon."

"What brings you here?"

The waiter arrived with her drink, and Jon took the opportunity to order an ale.

"Would you care to sit?" Angela offered.

He eyed her guardedly, then hooked a chair out and sat it astraddle. "So?"

"So." She ran her sweaty palms along her thighs. Where did one begin? For days she'd been trying to sort her thoughts, and finally she'd believed she had everything figured out, all the answers and explanations and reasons for her behavior. But now her mind felt like a jumbled attic. Suddenly the only thing she could think to say was, "I messed up."

His eyes drilled into her. "Yes, I know."

Angela felt her color deepen. "That's why I'm here. I'd like to apologize for the horrible things I said to you." She ducked her head. "They were childish and unfair, and I hope you didn't take them to heart."

Jon's ale arrived and he took a long sip before answering. "What did you expect? A guy tends to sit up and take notice when he's been told he's just taken all the joy out of his best friend's life." He set the glass down and again eyed her narrowly. Oh, he was hurt all right. She'd never seen him so reserved.

"The reason I said those things . . ." She paused, unsure of her ability to explain, because at the bottom of everything was the simple fact that she loved him.

"Suffice to say I've spent the last few days sorting priorities, and I'll be damned if . . ." Her eyes grew hot. "I'll be damned if you didn't come out right on top."

Jon started to say something.

"Please, let me finish before I lose courage." She sipped her drink. "It only occurred to me this week how serious you were about wanting to move back to Winston. I also realized how difficult I made that move. So I've tried to make amends."

He scowled. "Amends? How?"

"Well, I put a binder on the Thurgood house again, in your name. If you really, really don't want the place, fine, let it go. But, Jon, if you do, please, don't let someone else snatch it up."

Jon's eyebrows arched so high they practically disappeared under his hair.

"The second thing I did . . ." Here she took a much bigger sip of her schnapps. "I called Mrs. Conroy yesterday and asked if the board would reconsider your application for the WSO directorship."

"You what?" Jon stood up and turned his chair around.

"Poor woman got pretty confused. She'd offered me the job just the day before. But in the end she said yes. So . . ." Angela left the sentence open, but her meaning was obvious. The position was his for the taking.

Jon clutched his head in his hands, his eyes trained on hers. Was he angry? Was he about to tell her to get lost?

"Oh, Angel," he finally breathed. Just hearing him say her name flooded her with relief. "I told you I don't want the job, and I mean it. I'm perfectly happy with the one I've got. As you once said, I'm a musician, not a conductor. But the house—" he smiled unexpectedly "—now that's another matter. I will take you up on your offer—on one condition."

"What?" She'd agree to anything to make him happy.

Jon leaned closer. "That you move in with me."

Angela nearly toppled her drink. "What?"

"Give all that great old furniture you own a proper home."

"Oh. It's my furniture you want, is it?"

Jon's amusement deepened. "Yes. You know I don't have any, myself."

"You're making fun of me. I'm sorry. I came here in good faith, but maybe I should leave."

When she attempted to get up, however, Jon grabbed her wrist. "Angel, I'm making fun of both of us, not just you."

She searched his face, startled, confused.

"Sit down, sweetheart," he said tenderly. He moved his chair around to her side of the table and, turning his back to the room, carved out a private little space for them to talk. Then he took her hands in his, forcing her to face him squarely. "You see, you're not the only one who knows how to mess up, and when I do, I aim high. Mess-ups on a cosmic level."

Angela frowned. "What are you talking about?"

He sighed. "I was a fool for running off nine years ago. I should have talked to you, should have called or written and told you how much you meant to me." He looked aside, swallowed. "But I didn't."

"It's perfectly understandable. You were young. You were frightened and confused by what we'd done, and you had four years at Juilliard ahead of you, dreams to follow after that..."

"No. I made the wrong choice. I chose to chase a career, thinking it was a me-or-you situation. If I didn't put myself first, I thought, everything I'd ever dreamed of doing or becoming would go up in smoke."

"That just might've happened, Jon. Can you honestly say you'd be the same person today if you hadn't done what you did? The teachers you learned from, the broad range of musical experiences you enjoyed..."

Jon's grip on her hands tightened. "But there was no excuse for not staying in touch with you. I should've realized that a career and a love life are not mutually exclusive. But I didn't, and as time passed it become more and more difficult to call. For that, all I can say is I'm sorry.

"If it's any consolation, I was miserable. Memories of you wouldn't give me peace. Through nine years and four continents, I couldn't get you out of my mind. Finally I knew I had to return and find out what those memories were all about." He lifted one of her hands and pressed his lips to her palm.

Sitting on the edge of her seat, Angela shook her head, stupefied. "I don't believe this."

A frown troubled Jon's brow. "I'm sorry to hear that, but it's probably only what I deserve."

"No. When I say I don't believe this, I mean this is too good to be true."

A smile warmed his eyes. "Yeah?"

"Yeah."

He smiled more confidently. "Good. Because I finally figured it out." Oblivious to the people behind him, Jon threaded his fingers through her hair and pulled her closer. "What those memories were about, of course, was the fact that I love you. Always have. Always will." He moved in and kissed her lips.

Angela was sure she floated clear into the air, like one of the pretty balloons he'd given her. "Well, that's good to know, Mr. Stoddard," she replied dreamily, "because I happen to love you, too."

"Are you sure?"

"Very."

"What about this competitiveness you've driven me crazy with lately?"

"Oh, that." She wrinkled her nose. "Well, the long and short of it is, there is no competition, Jon. I only wanted to excel at something so you'd consider me your equal."

"Oh, Angel." Jon's expression was pained. "When have I ever not—"

She placed her fingers over his lips. "I know. If anything, you've always believed I could do far more than I actually could. There was only that one incident of rejection, and at eighteen, it cut deep. I thought if I'd been prettier and smarter, you wouldn't have left."

Jon was about to say something, but just at that moment, the saxophone player appeared at his side. "Sorry to interrupt, but it's that time again."

Jon sighed, his broad shoulders slumping. "Don't run off, sweetheart. We still have a lot to settle."

Angela watched him walk away and join the other musicians. When they began to play, she tried to pay attention, but she was wound much too tight with everything that had been said.

Jon, too, seemed unable to concentrate. His brow remained knit, his eyes troubled, and time and again he looked toward her table.

When the number finally ended, he got up from his piano and stepped over to the other musicians. They leaned in, nodding as he spoke, and watching them, Angela frowned. What was Jon plotting now? For a moment she tensed, thinking he might have another flute tucked under his piano. But no, he couldn't. He hadn't expected her tonight.

Jon returned to the piano and adjusted the microphone. Simultaneously the others stepped back, instruments lowered, like soldiers at ease. A hush fell over the audience as Jon gathered their attention, the silence deepening while he continued to stare at his hands poised over the keys. Finally, he said quite simply, ''This is for Angel.''

Angela sucked in her breath. For Angel? What was he doing? She was still confused when he began to play.

She recognized the piece immediately. How could she not? It was ''The Angel Waltz,'' Jon's dubious tribute to her, pretty much as it had sounded the first time she'd heard it when she was sixteen—simple, predictable and sweet. Angela couldn't believe Jon was playing it in public.

But almost imperceptibly the steady one-two-three rhythm began to change, the simple melody became layered, and before long Angela realized she was listening to an extremely complex jazz number—beautiful and intense and full of surprises. By the time Jon finished, she'd gone through three tissues, and her tears were still flowing.

Jon stood up and, ignoring the applause that broke over him, strode off the stage straight to Angela's table. ''Come on. Let's get out of here.'' He held her coat for her.

She sniffed. ''But the band...''

"Never mind the band. Let's go." He gripped her arm and escorted her to the door, earning the smiling curiosity of everyone they passed on the way.

Once outside, he wasted no time in wrapping her in his arms and covering her mouth with his. He was trembling— arms, chest, thighs. Even his lips had a certain desperation about them as they moved over hers.

"Angel, my Angel," he whispered.

"Yes, I'm here." She slipped her arms under his sports jacket and, working them up his muscled back, moved into him until they were a snug fit.

He drew in a sharp breath, closed his eyes and ran his parted lips along her hot cheek. "Sweetheart, we've got to do something about this friendship of ours."

Shuddering under his touch, she replied, "Do you have any suggestions?"

A slow sensual smile eased across his face. "What do you say we slap a license on it?"

"What sort?" Her voice was suddenly breathless. "Hunting? Fishing?"

"Maybe later. Right now I'm thinking more in terms of marriage."

"Marriage." She closed her eyes, wanting to cry all over again. "You mean the kind with a house and a dog and . . . and children?"

"Oh, at least enough children for a string quartet."

Her throat worked convulsively. "I think we can work something out."

Jon stood very still. "Is that a yes?" All his flippancy was gone.

So was hers. "Yes."

Jon closed his eyes and held her so close she could barely breathe. "Thank God. I never want to be apart from you again."

"You won't be, I promise," she somehow got out.

"Good, because without you . . ." Jon pulled back, smoothing her long hair from her flushed face. "Oh, my Angel, my soul . . ." He leaned in and kissed her again, a long possessive kiss that made her forget they were standing on a public sidewalk.

"I know," she murmured. "Without you, I feel empty, too, as if half of me is missing."

"We're really fortunate, aren't we? What we share is a very special love."

She smiled, another tear slipping down her cheek. "One of cosmic proportions is my estimation."

"At the very least."

In the distance across the river, fireworks had been booming for some time.

"Must be close to midnight," Jon murmured.

"Mmm. Can we see the fireworks from here?"

"I'm not sure." Jon drew her to his side and walked to the corner. From there they discovered they could indeed see the display, at least the uppermost splashes of it. But despite the sky's filling with brilliant jets of color, Angela and Jon remained absorbed in each other.

"You haven't told me what you think of the completed 'Angel Waltz.'"

Angela purposely hemmed and hawed. "It's okay." When she saw how crestfallen he looked, she laughed and hugged him close. "It was magnificent, and I'm not just saying that because I was flattered. Jon—" she was filled with wonder "—you've become one heck of a composer."

He winked. "The best is yet to come."

"I haven't a doubt."

"For you, too, sweetheart. You're one heck of a conductor." Grinning mischievously, he kissed her forehead. "You know—"

She laid a hand on his jacket. "Stop. I don't like the sound of that 'you know.'"

The sky began to pulse with a series of explosions so thick and frequent it could only mean the grand finale was under way.

"You know," he persisted, the fireworks reflected in his deep midnight eyes, "I play with this little band over in Boston, and I was just thinking..."

"No, don't think, Jon."

"I was just thinking that someday I might be able to wrangle an invitation for you to lead that little band as guest conductor."

"No, Jon. I'm not interested in conducting the Boston Symphony Orchestra. The only group I plan to conduct from now on is the WSO. You're out of your mind. You always have been. . . ."

Before she could say another word, he kissed her. "Happy New Year, Angel."

From behind restaurant doors and apartment windows drifted the muffled jangling of noisemakers, cheers and sentimental strains of "Auld Lang Syne."

Angela's eyes misted. "Happy... First Night, Jon," she whispered.

With his arm around her shoulders, they slowly walked back toward the club. "What do you say I grab my coat and we cut out now?" suggested Jon.

"Sounds good to me. Where do you want to go?"

"Well, how about you help me pack my things—it shouldn't take long—and then we head up to Winston?"

Angela beamed from ear to ear.

At the door to the club Jon paused to kiss her one more time. When he finally lifted his head, he smiled at her, his eyes sparkling with love. Angela returned his smile, aware of how blessedly happy she was. Life with this wonderful man was never going to be dull. Of course, she'd probably never feel surefooted or in control of anything again. But then, who ever did? Life was uncertain, surprises and challenges at every turn—if you were lucky. The best a person could hope for was to find someone to join hands with while taking the glorious ride.

"I love you, Angel," Jon whispered in her ear.

"Love you, too," she replied.

Then he opened the door, and with fingers reaching to intertwine, they walked through.

Let
HARLEQUIN ROMANCE®
take you

BACK TO THE

Come to the Diamond B Ranch,
near Fawn Creek, Arizona.

Meet Seth Brody, rancher. *And* Janna Whitley, city girl.
He's one man who's hard to impress. And she's a woman
with a lot to prove.

Read THE TENDERFOOT by Patricia Knoll,
January's hilarious Back to the Ranch title!

Available wherever Harlequin books are sold.

RANCH8

NEW YORK TIMES **Bestselling Author**

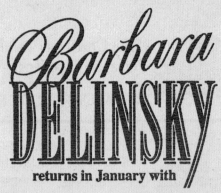

Barbara
DELINSKY

returns in January with

THE REAL THING

Stranded on an island off the coast of Maine,
Deirdre Joyce and Neil Hersey got the
solitude they so desperately craved—
but they also got each other, something they
hadn't expected. Nor had they expected
to be consumed by a desire so powerful
that the idea of living alone again was
unimaginable. A marrige of "convenience"
made sense—or did it? B0B7

HARLEQUIN®

Make Christmas a truly
Romantic experience—with

HARLEQUIN ROMANCE®

Wouldn't *you* love to kiss a tall, dark
Texan under the mistletoe? Gwen does,
in HOME FOR CHRISTMAS by
Ellen James. Share the experience!

Wouldn't *you* love to kiss a sexy
New Englander on a snowy Christmas
morning? Angela does, in Shannon
Waverly's CHRISTMAS ANGEL.
Share the experience!

Look for both of these Christmas
Romance titles, available in December
wherever Harlequin Books are sold.

(And don't forget that Romance novels
make great gifts! Easy to buy, easy to
wrap and just the right size for a
stocking stuffer. And they make a
wonderful treat when you need a break
from Christmas shopping, Christmas
wrapping and stuffing stockings!)

©DG 1990

HRXT

HARLEQUIN ROMANCE®

WELCOME BACK, MARGARET WAY!

After an absence of five years, Margaret Way—one of our most popular authors ever—returns to Romance!

Start the New Year with the excitement and passion of

ONE FATEFUL SUMMER
A brand-new Romance from Margaret Way

Available in January wherever Harlequin Books are sold.

HRMW

When the only time you have for yourself is…

Christmas is such a busy time—with shopping, decorating, writing cards, trimming trees, wrapping gifts.…

When you do have a few *stolen moments* to call your own, treat yourself to a brand-new *short* novel. Relax with one of our Stocking Stuffers— or with all six!

Each STOLEN MOMENTS title is a complete and original contemporary romance that's the perfect length for the busy woman of the nineties! Especially at Christmas…

And they make perfect **stocking stuffers**, too! (For your mother, grandmother, daughters, friends, co-workers, neighbors, aunts, cousins—all the other women in your life!)

Look for the STOLEN MOMENTS display in December

STOCKING STUFFERS:

HIS MISTRESS Carrie Alexander
DANIEL'S DECEPTION Marie DeWitt
SNOW ANGEL Isolde Evans
THE FAMILY MAN Danielle Kelly
THE LONE WOLF Ellen Rogers
MONTANA CHRISTMAS Lynn Russell

HSM2

WORLDWIDE LIBRARY ®